The Magick of New Beginnings

Book Four in the Wise Woman Series

EMaddex

Elaine Gugin Maddex

For permission, please email the author at:
guginmaddex@gmail.com

Bookstores and wholesale orders can be placed with the author
at guginmaddex@gmail.com

Website: elaineguginmaddex.com

Maddex, Elaine Gugin, author

Cover art design by Chris Tyreman

Issued in print and electronic formats.
ISBN 978-1-987982-49-7 (paperback).
ISBN 978-1-987982-50-3 (epub)

DISCLAIMER
This is a work of fiction. Any names and characters are used
fictitiously or are the product of the author's imagination. Any
resemblance to actual persons, living or dead, is entirely coin-
cidental. Places and events are a combination of fictitious and
real.

 Team Published
with Artistic Warrior Publishing
artisticwarrior.com

To my hometown of Minnedosa, Manitoba.
Thank you for my family roots, my childhood friends,
and my magickal memories.
I am because of my beginnings.
Without you there would be no stories to tell.

Table of Contents

The Magick of New Beginnings

Elaine Gugin Maddex

Irish Blessing
For Wee Ones

May the good Lord protect our wee ones so dear.

May their guardian angels be always near.

Bless them as they grow and play.

Grace them with your love day by day.

1
Big News

Tessy McGuigan dreamily gazed out the kitchen window of her charming Victorian home, Ashling Manor. It was hard to believe she'd lived in Saskatchewan for over thirty-five years now.

As she set the kettle on the stove for tea, her mind wandered to memories of when she first moved to Ladyslipper. She stepped off the train a young lass eager and ready to begin her teaching career. She met her late husband, Dermot, soon after. They were both elementary school teachers and you could say it was love at first sight. They married within a year. When they purchased Ashling Manor a few years later, it was a dream come true.

Tessy sighed. Dermot's been gone almost six years already. Where did the time go? A smile twitched on her lips. Grand memories, those. And now here she was married to Marshall, another wonderful man. She felt she'd been truly blessed.

The sound of the kettle whistle broke her thoughts. On her way to the stove, she glanced out the window and chuckled as she noticed her two canine companions, Duke and Darby. They darted here and there sniffing out all the fresh scents that spawned overnight.

Tessy didn't know why she woke with a sense of excitement that morning. She was in a chipper mood. She looked over at her two lethargic felines, Merlin and Cordelia, and then addressed them. "What better season could there be than autumn?"

They ignored her enthusiasm and remained curled up in their basket soaking in the warm sunbeams that streamed through the window.

Tessy poured boiling water over an herbal concoction of nettle and raspberry leaves she'd gathered from her garden. She threw in a few dried cranberries and whole cloves to add a burst of seasonal flare.

It was sunny and unusually warm for Tessy's best-loved time of year. Still, there was a nip of crispness in the fall air. She took her tea and a blanket out to the picnic chair by the fire pit. She also brought her photo album. She set the album and her tea down on the arm of the chair and snuggly wrapped the blanket around her and sat. She took in a long deep breath. "Oh, how I love the smell of autumn."

The dogs waited impatiently by her side, each competing for rubs and her attention. Complying with their wishes, she scolded, "Now, be careful, the pair of ye, or you'll be spilling my tea." Once the dogs had their fill of affection, they went off to play in the yard.

Tessy quieted herself and went into mindful meditation and sincere gratitude for this day and what it would have to offer. When she was done, she savoured her tea while she looked through the photo album and reminisced. It was just over a year ago that she and Marshall were in Ireland on their honeymoon. It seemed like only yesterday. They had a glorious time on that holiday. The months that followed had been just as glorious, even though they were filled with busy.

In the past year, Doctor Marshall Tayse had fully retired from his general practice in Winnipeg. They were still in the process of renovating Marshall's large home into a B&B, called the Doctor's Inn. Marshall's dear house staff, Dotty and Bert Mitchell, would manage and run it for them so Marshall could return home to Tessy.

Tessy looked up and smiled at the rather new, large Quonset at the back end of her property. It was referred to as the shop by Tessy and as Brigid's domain to Marshall. Brigid was Marshall's new retirement hobby: rebuilding a 1929 Ford Model A, he lovingly dubbed Brigid. Tessy knew this would be where she'd find Marshall if he ever went missing.

The past year was also filled with the constant comings and goings of their beautiful grandchildren, their family and friends. Aye, busy, was the only way to describe this past year.

Tessy sat quiet for quite some time, enjoying the ambiance of fall. She smiled as she watched the leaves frolic and dance to the ground. She was lost in the moment when the phone rang. Tessy untangled herself from the blanket as quickly as possible, but she still missed the call.

After Marshall moved in, he insisted they get new phones with call display and a message feature on them. Tessy was still quite in awe of this not-so-new technology.

Blessed be, she thought. It was Sage who had called. She smiled and hit redial, last caller. Sage answered right away.

* * *

"Hello."

"Morning, Sage dear. It's Tessy. I see ye called. How are ye doing?"

"Hi Tess. We're doing great. How are you?"

"Grand, thank ye, dear."

"Oh, good. I was just wondering if you're going to be home for the next little while?"

"Aye, dear, I am."

"I was hoping to drop by," Sage said, "if you're not busy."

"Aye, that would be lovely. Pop on by anytime."

"Is now okay?"

"Now would be grand."

"Perfect. See you in a few minutes. Bye."

"Bye, love."

Sage smiled as she readied herself to go to Tessy's. Ever since she'd arrived in Ladyslipper the spring before, Tessy had been there for her. They bumped into each other by accident and neither of their lives had been the same since. To make it even more interesting they discovered they were related. They had a magickal connection that literally sparked the moment they touched hands. Tessy took Sage under her wing and when Tessy returned from her honeymoon in Ireland, she guided Sage in the teachings and mystical ways of their Celtic heritage.

Remembering all this put an extra bounce in her step. She couldn't wait to share the big news with Tessy. Tessy was her mentor and like her second mom. She was one of the most important people in Sage's life and she wanted her to be one of the first to know.

Sage thought back to all the wonderful things that had happened since her arrival in Ladyslipper. Finding Tessy and opening her alternative healing shop, The Healing Sage, was like a dream come true. Then, meeting and dating Tommy Bracken shortly after she arrived was magickal. Marrying him, a few short months ago, put the icing on the cake. She knew the move to Ladyslipper was her destiny.

Sage reached the front gate to Ashling Manor. Darby and Duke looked up from playing a savage game of tug-o'-war with a large, knotted rope. She laughed as they simultaneously dropped it when they spotted her and ran to welcome their guest. She lavished them with pets and rubs as they accompanied her to the front door.

* * *

Tessy looked up when she heard Sage come through the front door. "I'm in the kitchen, dear," Tessy called. Sage made her way down the hall and into the kitchen. They greeted with a loving hug.

"How grand to see ye, dear. Come sit. Would ye like a tea, love?"

"Sure, that would be great. Thanks. Where's Marshall?" Sage asked as she made her way to the table.

"Off to Winnipeg. There are some plumbing problems at the B&B he wants to oversee." Tessy poured hot water over the fragrant herbs in her teapot.

"Oh, that's too bad. Hope it's nothing major."

"Aye. That makes two of us."

"How are Dotty and Bert making out? Do they like the idea of running an inn?"

"Aye. They seem to. Well, ye know how Dotty loves to fuss. And the good Lord knows, once Bert gets to know ye he does love to chat and visit. He can tell stories like no other. The only man I know that could out-do him 'twould be my twin brother, Keenan, over in Ireland. Now, if ever there was a man packed full of the Blarney, 'tis Keenan!"

They both laughed knowing there was more truth in that statement than either of them cared to admit.

Tessy placed the teapot and a plate of rhubarb muffins on the table between the two of them and sat down. She took one look at Sage and smiled. Tessy could see Sage was lost in absent concentration and ready to burst with some kind of news. She reached over and patted Sage's hand.

"Now, dear, I can see you've something on your mind. What is it ye have to say?"

Sage lowered her head and when she raised it, she was beaming. She hesitated, bit her bottom lip, then exploded with the news.

"We're pregnant!"

Tessy leapt off her chair and gathered Sage in her arms. "Oh, my sweet girl, how absolutely marvellous. Congratulations!"

"Thanks. It's a little sooner than we expected but we're so excited and couldn't be happier."

Tessy reached into her apron pocket to retrieve a hanky and dabbed her eyes and nose before she spoke again. "Oh, this is just wonderful news," she repeated. "What did your mam have to say?"

Sage sheepishly put her head down. "Well, actually, we haven't told her yet."

"Why on earth not, dear?"

"Well, we just found out for sure yesterday after I peed on the stick. I knew she was going to be busy running errands and setting up for her annual fall fundraiser this weekend so thought I'd wait until later to tell her. And to be honest, I don't think she's going to be quite so thrilled."

"Oh, Sage dear, why would ye say that? This will be her first grandchild. I'm sure she'll be ecstatic."

"Well, we're hoping, but you know she wasn't crazy about Tommy and I getting married so quickly to begin with. And now I'm pregnant. I think she's going to flip."

"Sage, ye can't think that. 'Tis a miracle. Every child is. I think your mam will be more understanding than ye know."

"Well, I certainly hope she feels that way. After her terrible marriage to my dad, she's a little skeptical about all relationships. But I promise I'll call her tonight."

"Aye, I think that a grand idea. I'm sure she'll be tickled pink. So, you'll be planning a spring baby, then? How precious."

"Yep. But not sure of an exact date yet. I booked an appointment with the doctor and we're hoping to have our first ultrasound soon."

Tessy smiled, closed her eyes, and gently grasped her heart, visualizing the sweet little bundle. Suddenly, her eyes flew open. She immediately recalled the premonition from last year. She had a vivid dream of Sage and Tommy's parenthood; however, in this dream there had been two wee bundles. Twins.

Sage noticed Tessy's change in demeanour. "Tessy, what is it?"

Tessy snapped back to reality. "Oh, nothing, love. I was just thinking how busy your life is about to get." She was not ready to share the apparition with Sage. If she hadn't even seen the doctor yet, far be it for her to break the news.

"That's for sure." Sage laughed. "And I've already been quite queasy for the last week or so. I've had to excuse myself from my clients a time or two. Tommy says I should cut back my schedule a bit. I really don't want to, but I just might have to."

"Probably wouldn't be a bad idea, my dear."

"Well, thank goodness Tommy is working full time at the auto repair shop. They seem to really like him. They said because of his certification in farm mechanics they're lucky to have him."

"Indeed, they are," Tessy boasted. She had grown to love Tommy as a son and was so proud of him. When he came to town as a young drifter after losing his mom, Tessy befriended and guided him. Knowing she had her hand in introducing Tommy and Sage did her heart good. And now here he was married to her distant cousin and about to be a father. Blessed be.

They drank their tea and merrily chatted about babies and new beginnings. Before Sage left, Tessy popped into her herbal kitchen and mixed up a special Mommy-to-be tea blend to help with Sage's morning sickness. When Tessy returned to the main kitchen with the tin, Sage got up from the table.

"I guess I had better get going. The auto repair shop is only open until noon on Saturday, so Tommy should be home soon."

"All right, love. Now ye make sure ye give me a call if ye need anything day or night. We must take special care of you and those wee babes."

"Babies!" A wide-eyed Sage gasped.

"Oh, sorry, love. I don't know where that came from." Tessy quickly backpedaled and couldn't believe what she had just spilled.

"Oh! I didn't even think of that! Can you imagine?"

"Oh, love, don't pay me any mind. That just fell out of me mouth without thinkin'. I'm sure all is just fine."

Sage laughed. "Okay. But can you imagine?" she repeated. She took the tin Tessy handed her, and they hugged.

Tessy walked her out to the main road and watched her skip down the footpath until she was out of sight. While Tessy watched Sage disappear, she scolded herself for making such a huge blunder. She would be careful not to let that slip again until the doctor confirmed what Tessy already knew to be true.

2
Calling of the Clan

Tessy was so happy for Sage and Tommy. She was quite excited to know that soon there would be wee poppets for her to cuddle and spoil. She and her late husband, Dermot, had never been blessed with children. Therefore, she missed out on the joy of infants, the coos, the giggles, the smell of a freshly bathed baby. Oh, how she was looking forward to it all, even changing nappies. Tessy smiled.

She wondered whether she should call Marshall and share the good news. "Hmmm, I best wait until Sage talks to her mother before I start spreading the word," she said out loud to the now alert Merlin. He licked his paw then rubbed it across his face.

As Tessy washed the teacups and tidied up the kitchen, she could think of little else other than babies. Her thoughts rolled back to the note written in Gaelic and the amulet and ring left by her mother more than four decades ago. Tessy's mam's maiden name was Haggerty and so was Sage's. In Sage's clan of Haggertys, the females especially, were all named after herbs.

"I wonder if Sage will carry on the tradition," she said to Merlin, who continued to ignore her. Then, remembering a part of the sacred, mysterious note she recited aloud, "Find the clan named after the herbs, for they are the protected ones with powerful words."

Sage was making great strides in learning the wondrous ways of a true Wise Woman, but Tessy had not yet shared the note with her. She decided the time was drawing near to enlighten her student.

* * *

Not wanting to waste another moment of this lovely fall day inside, Tessy grabbed a couple of wicker baskets and set out to gather the dregs of her remaining herbs. She had already gathered and dried most everything during their prime to use in the kitchen. She also divided and potted what she needed fresh for indoors during the winter months ahead. What was left she would bundle and dry for either smudging or sacred rituals.

She snipped and plucked, leaving a few late fading blooms for the chubby bumblebees to gather and store the last dribbles of nectar. Tessy loved the way Mother Earth provided for all her offspring. She smiled, realizing Sage had just blossomed from Maiden to Mother and she, too, was now providing nourishment for the tiny seeds she carried within. "Oh, how blessed the cycle of life." Tessy softly tittered as she watched a fat bumblebee dig its way into the centre of a flowering red clover.

Tessy finished in the garden and puttered about filling bird feeders and baths. It was late afternoon when she went inside the house. She was preparing supper when the phone rang.

"Good evening, to ye."

"Hi Tess. It's Sage."

"Well, hello dear. How are ye feeling?"

"Great. Thanks. I thought I'd let you know that I just got off the phone with Mom."

"How did she take the news, dear?"

"Well, she was pretty shocked at first, but she did seem to come around after we spoke for a while. The longer we spoke the more excited she was, especially when she figured out we will have a spring baby. She even said she'd come and help out."

"That's grand, dear. I knew she'd be thrilled. She just needed a minute to catch her breath, 'tis all. Do ye feel better now that you've told her?"

"Oh, yes, so much better. Tommy's really glad, too. He's so excited he wants to shout it to the whole world." Sage giggled.

"Isn't that sweet, dear?" Tessy chuckled. "So ye won't mind me sharing the news with Marshall, then?"

"No, not at all. We're going to try and keep it a secret around town until we see the doctor and make sure everything is good to go."

"Aye, of course, dear. Consider our lips buttoned."

"Thanks, Tessy. Well, I'd better get going. Tommy just went out to the balcony to take the burgers off the barbecue."

"All right, love. Say hi to Tommy and wish him hearty congratulations for me. Have a grand evening. Bye for now."

Tessy took her tea into the library after she finished her supper. Earlier in the day she had retrieved her dream journal from her bedside stand, brought it downstairs and placed it on the large mahogany desk. She set her teacup next to the notebook and sat in the matching desk chair. She started the journal while in Ireland on her honeymoon. She wanted to record the strange dreams she experienced there. Most of those dreams turned out to be channelled messages from her deceased mother. They guided Tessy to the long-standing mystery regarding her parents' death at the hands of her estranged cousin, Agnes Haggerty. However, some dreams were of the Haggerty Clan. Mostly those named after the herbs, like her dear Sage. Those messages were the ones Tessy was most interested in researching.

While thumbing through the notes and recorded visions, Tessy sipped the fragrant tea, deep in thought. She had thoroughly researched and studied this particular clan of Haggerty's in as much detail as possible during the past year. There wasn't much information available and there were many blanks yet to be filled.

Tessy hoped when Sage's mother, Rosemary, and her grandmother, Rose, were in town for Sage and Tommy's wedding, they might be able to shine some light on their ancestry. Even though they were able to fill in a few of the blanks for Tessy there were still many questions to this ancient puzzle.

Tessy planned on inviting them both back for a visit. She hoped to gather enough information to do some investigating as to where and why the name tradition started.

She also wanted to see if either of them knew anything regarding the amulet and ring. She'd had her mother's Gaelic note translated while in Ireland. She discovered the amulet and ring were centuries old and handed down only to gifted

Haggertys who'd bore twins. That explained how her mother had ended up with them. That was as much as she knew and there were still so many unanswered questions. It was time to get some answers regarding this ancient puzzle and Tessy felt her student, Sage, should be included in the unravelling.

It was late when Tessy finally turned in. She was tired, but still tossed from one side to the other, flipping her pillow in the hopes of that somehow helping. She couldn't get the mystery out of her mind. Even though she had pondered over it, from time to time, it didn't consume her as it did tonight. She was sure it was because of Sage's pregnancy. She felt these precious little twins deserved to know the answers that she and Keenan never got.

Tessy untangled the bedsheets wrapped around her and got up to make some warm milk and honey. She put on her housecoat, wriggled her toes into her slippers, and headed to the kitchen.

While she stirred the heating mixture she resolved, right then, that she would invite Rosemary and Rose for another visit. She also decided it was time to unveil the amulet, ring, and Gaelic note to Sage. Confident with her two big decisions she drank her relaxing mixture and made her way back up to bed. With her mind now calmed, she snuggled down and slipped into a peaceful sleep.

She woke early with a smile twitching at her lips. She had dreamt of her homeland. She believed she'd heard her twin brother's rooster shrilling as it did every early dawn while they were there. Tessy giggled to herself. Oh, how Marshall had complained about those abrupt awakenings.

She was up and going in good time. She peeked outside to see the day looked cloudy and cool. She felt especially hungry, and considering the day, she concluded a traditional Irish breakfast would be in order. Oddly enough, she always enjoyed coffee, not tea, when she cooked a full breakfast. She got it brewing first, then pulled out the sausages and eggs from the fridge and wondered what she would prepare for supper. A stew would be nice. She put the sausages on, poured herself a coffee, and opened the latest flyer from Kessel's Grocery. After leafing through the flyer, she got up to flip the sausages. Before she could sit down again, the phone rang.

She picked up the phone and gave her usual cheerful greeting. "Good mornin' to ye!"

"Good morning, sweetheart."

"Marshall, love! How are ye?"

"Pretty good. But I sure wish I could say the same for my plumbing."

"Oh dear. That doesn't sound good."

"Nope, it's definitely not. I just thought I'd give you a quick call and let you know, looks like I won't be home for a while, yet."

"Oh, I'm sorry, love. Well, don't worry your mind about anything here. Everything is just as fine as frog's fur."

"Okay, darling. I'm sorry. I miss you so much. I promise I'll be home as soon as we get this figured out."

"All right, love. Now, make sure ye call on Archangel Michael for help. He has an incredible knack for fixing any mechanical, technical, and even plumbing problems. Among many other wondrous miracles, of course.

Marshall chuckled. "Okay, I'll make sure to do that. Thanks. Well, better go, dear. I love you." He was about to hang up.

"Marshall, love! Wait! I've something exciting to tell ye and I just can't wait any longer."

"Oh, sorry. What's up?"

"Sage and Tommy are going to have a baby!" She opted to avoid the plural version.

"What? Wow, that's wonderful. Good for them. Please give them my best wishes if you see them before I get home."

"Aye, love. I will. But maybe just keep it between us for now, if ye don't mind."

"Okay, honey. Well, I hate to cut this short, but the plumber just arrived."

"All right, love. Good luck. I'll be sending ye an Irish blessing along with some positive energy. I love ye. Talk to ye soon."

Tessy hung up and took a sip of coffee. "Poor Marshall."

The sausage was done, so Tessy popped a couple of eggs in the pan. She plated up her breakfast, took it to the table, and enjoyed every morsel. When she was done, she tidied up the kitchen.

The weather didn't look like it was going to turn nice anytime soon, so she headed straight to her library and switched on the computer. She got comfortably seated and typed in her password.

It was time for research. She found her favourite genealogy site and typed in Haggerty. She was bound and determined to find some trace of the Clan's history. And, hopefully, about the amulet and ring that had caused such torment, not to mention many sleepless nights.

3
Traces of History

Tessy spent most of the day scrolling and filtering through clans of Haggertys on different genealogy sites and taking notes. Finally, she believed she'd made a slight breakthrough. She discovered an early clan with names mostly representing magickal herbs. "Oh, how exciting!" She beamed over at her massive black cat, Merlin. He was sprawled across the corner of the mahogany desk. Merlin, however, did not appear to share in Tess's joyous revelation. He stretched and repositioned himself with his back towards her.

"Humph, thanks a lot." Tessy playfully scowled. Her eyes were tired, so she decided to take a break. She got up, stroked the cat on her way by, leaving the door open so Merlin could leave when finished with his nap.

She steeped some tea and fixed herself a salmon sandwich. Tessy looked out at the blustery fall day while she ate. The dogs played their game of choice: tug-o'-war. She smiled at their competitive nature.

It didn't take long for the smell of salmon to rustle Merlin from his perch. He skidded around the corner and into the kitchen with the exuberance of a kitten.

Tessy laughed. "Oh sure, so now ye want to be my friend!" She placed the empty can on the floor for Merlin to lick clean.

Cordelia, who was more elusive, was outside, undoubtedly in the old garage. She would be curled up on her favourite cushion soaking up the sun yet safely sheltered from the autumn breeze. Tessy would give her a special treat later. She tried never to show favouritism between her beloved pets.

Tessy glanced up at the clock and almost spat her tea back into the cup. "Great leaping Leprechauns!" she blurted. It was almost three in the afternoon. She hadn't realized she'd been staring at the computer screen all day. "Well, now what am I to do?" she asked Merlin. "I just had my lunch and 'tis almost supper. Guess 'twill be a light Sunday supper for me tonight." Merlin looked at her and licked his whiskers as she put her dirty dishes in the sink.

Tessy went back into the library, sorted through her notes for a short time, then turned off the computer. She needed some fresh air and wanted to get outside before the sun got any lower.

Tessy pulled a light tuque over her swept up curls, tossed on one of her heaviest wraps and headed out to the back yard. The autumn smells were euphoric. Tessy stopped to take it all in. She closed her eyes, raised her nostrils, and sniffed the air releasing the wild woman deep within her soul. The dogs spotted her and immediately sprang to her side. Even the constant muzzle nudging could not break Tessy's primeval state of concentration. Thousands of years ran through her inner being, knowing her ancestors breathed in that very same sweet scent. No other time of year proclaimed such a tantalizing bouquet. *Who would have thought that decaying vegetation could smell so heavenly?* she wondered. She allowed herself to drift back to reality.

She tussled with Duke and Darby for a few moments before they accompanied her on a walk. They headed straight for the wooded area behind Ashling Manor. Tessy wandered the leaf-covered path drinking in every divine encounter. The dogs, on the other hand, ventured into the brush to sniff out all the delicious foreign scents. They meandered for about an hour and got back to the house just as the sun was low. Streaming beams of harvest gold broke through the clouds. The glow was magickal.

When they reached the yard, the dogs immediately ran to a large, galvanized tub for a well-deserved drink of water. Surveying their kingdom was satisfying, but thirsty business. By the time Tessy opened the kitchen door they were right behind her and ready to come in.

"All right, then. Let's get ye fed." Tessy smiled. "You pups have had a mighty full day."

She took off her tuque, ruffled her hair and removed her wrap. She got all the animals fed and went to the fridge to see what she might have. As she suspected, she wasn't overly hungry, even after her long jaunt. She stood peering for a moment, weighing all her options. Then she pulled out a bowl. "Aye! The rest of this leftover hamburger soup will do just dandy."

While she was waiting for it to heat, she wondered how Marshall had made out. "The poor dear," she said out loud to Cordelia, who had finished eating and was now licking her paw to clean off her face. Tessy made a mental note to remember to somehow sneak Cordelia a little treat before bedtime. "If these repairs keep up, I fear Marshall will regret turning his home into a B&B."

She poured the steaming soup into a lovely wide rimmed bowl and sat at the kitchen table. The hearty soup smelled delicious and Tessy's appetite suddenly improved. There wasn't a dribble left when she was done.

Tessy took her tea into the library and retrieved her earlier notes on the clan named after herbs. As near as she could decipher, this clan was similar to her relatives. They also started out in the north of Ulster then migrated south. She hadn't been able to find the exact connection yet, so she decided that would be her quest tomorrow.

Tessy was more determined than ever to find answers. She picked up the phone to call Sage's mother, Rosemary, and invite her to Ladyslipper. She looked at the clock and calculated the time in Ontario. *Hmm, too late to call tonight. I'll call first thing in the mornin'.* She placed the phone back in its cradle.

She was on her way into the living room to get comfy and watch some TV when the phone rang.

"Good evenin' to ye," she answered.

"Tessy, it's Sage. I'm bleeding!" She sobbed into the phone.

"I'll be right there, love!"

4
A Frightful Ordeal

Tessy sprinted into her herbal kitchen. She pulled down jars of herbs, bottles of tinctures and bags of roots from the shelves of her healing sanctuary. She placed them in a tote, grabbed her car keys and was gone. She parked her car behind the Healing Sage and flew up the stairs to Sage and Tommy's flat. Tommy met her at the door. Tessy immediately noticed his bloodshot eyes and stress lines on his forehead. Sage wept uncontrollably on the couch

"I, I didn't know what to do," Tommy stammered.

"It will be fine, dear. Why don't ye go down and get some fresh air and leave Sage and I to chat for a mite?"

"Oh, I don't know, Tess." Tommy looked over at his distraught wife. She raised a hand, waved and nodded in agreement.

"Okay, if you're sure, babe." He walked over and kissed the top of her head. Sage reached up and squeezed his hand.

After he left, Tessy sat close to Sage, and they hugged. Tess, eventually, gently leaned Sage back and handed her a tissue.

"Now, dry your eyes and tell me what's happened. How much are ye bleeding?"

Sage got up and motioned for Tessy to follow her into the bedroom. She reached into the laundry basket and pulled out a pair of panties. Tessy strained to see the pale pink stain and tried to hide her overwhelming relief.

"Oh Sage, love. I think all is fine. That's just a bit of discharge, 'tis all. 'Tis quite normal at this stage."

"Really?" Sage brightened and dabbed her nose.

"Aye, love. When are ye to see your doctor?"

"My appointment is at 10:50 a.m. tomorrow with, Marshall's son, Dr. Kyle Tayse."

"Well, that's grand. I'm sure he'll confirm all is well. He's a wonderful, young doctor and we are so lucky to have him. Now then, I'm going to make ye a nice cup of that lovely nettle and ginger tea. Once ye drink that, ye head off to bed and get some rest. Ye'll feel much better in the mornin'"

Tessy got Sage calmed down with her cup of tea. She then went to scout out and have a wee chat with poor, rattled Tommy.

When she found him, she explained everything as best she could, trying to keep his level of embarrassment to a minimum. Tommy was pretty young yet and, what he considered woman's issues, still made him squirm. But, Tessy knew his un-measurable love for Sage. Even with Tommy not having a father figure in his life to show him the way, she knew he would master fatherhood beyond every expectation.

* * *

Ashling Manor was dark when Tessy walked in the front door. She flicked on the lights and let out a long sigh of relief. She stepped into the living room to just sit for a minute. She had already made up her mind to stop in at the Ladyslipper library the next day with the intent to pick up some good prenatal books for Sage and Tommy. With this being their first pregnancy they were going to need all the help they could get. *As with any young couple*, she smiled.

She got up and went to the kitchen to let the dogs out for their last runabout. Merlin scooted out behind them. She looked over to see Cordelia curled up in her basket. Ah, the perfect moment to sneak in that treat for her.

Tessy retrieved a spoon and a saucer, went to the fridge, and scooped out a little leftover salmon. She placed it down close to her and giggled when Cordelia sprang up and sprinted over to it. It certainly didn't take her long to devour her treat.

Tessy let the dogs in and stood waiting for Merlin to make up his mind as to whether he was spending the night in or out. He finally opted for in.

"Well, good night to ye all. Sweet dreams." With that, she switched off the light and headed to bed herself.

Relieved that Sage and Tommy's emergency turned out to be a false alarm, Tessy was able to comfortably fall into a deep sleep.

5
An Exasperating Customer for Jim Tucker

Right after breakfast, Tessy went into the den and looked up Rosemary's phone number and dialled. She wanted to extend her invitation and give her a hearty congratulations regarding the news of a blessed grandchild on the way.

Tessy heard the phone ring four times before there was a pleasant, "Hello."

"Hello. Is this Rosemary?"

"Yes. Tessy?"

"Aye, dear. How are ye?"

"Fine, thank you. What a lovely surprise. It's so nice to hear your voice."

"Aye, and yours. How are Rowan and Saffron doing?"

"Great, thanks. Rowan just started a new job he loves and Saffron is getting top marks in college. They couldn't be better."

"Ahh, that's grand to hear. I just wanted to call and congratulate you all on your wonderful news."

"Yes, I'm going to be a grandmother!" Rosemary gushed. "And, Rowan and Saffron can't wait to have a niece or nephew to spoil."

"Aye, such an exciting time, to be sure."

"Yes, I just wish we lived closer so we could be there for her."

"I would imagine. Well, be rest assured, we're here for both her and Tommy. No matter what."

"Thank you, Tess. You have no idea how reassuring that is."

"Our pleasure, dear. Say, there's another reason for my calling. I was wondering if ye and your mother would like to come for a visit? We could make it a surprise for Sage, if ye like?"

"Oh Tessy! That would be wonderful. And, I have some time off I'm to use up fairly quick. So, how perfect."

"Grand. And your mam?"

"I'm sure she would love to join me."

"Grand! Also, when Rose was here last, she mentioned she'd gathered some genealogy and other information on your Haggerty ancestry. Do ye think she would mind bringing that along with her? I thought we might take a look and see what we can come up with as far as our connecting heritage."

"I'm positive she would enjoy spending some time going over all that information with you."

"Oh my, that would be marvellous. Well, please ask her to bring it with you, then."

"You bet. Well, I'll start getting things arranged and let you know as soon as I have a date for the flight. Thanks again. I'm so excited. And yes, I think it would be fun to keep it a surprise for Sage."

"Grand. Well, I'll look forward to hearing from ye soon, then. Have a lovely week and give my best to Rowan and Saffron for me. And, of course, to your dear mam."

Tessy was thrilled to have Rosemary and Rose coming for a

visit. She loved having Ashling Manor filled with guests.

When Tessy hung up it was just after nine. She ran upstairs to get dressed and headed off to the Ladyslipper library. She wanted to drop off the prenatal books for Sage and Tommy before their doctor's appointment. She was also anxious to see how Sage was feeling.

Tessy found a couple of excellent books that would help guide Sage and Tommy along on their journey to parenthood. She arrived at their apartment to find both Sage and Tommy in good spirits and excited about their appointment.

Tessy carried on down to the pharmacy where she had a selection of her herbs, lotions, and potions. The Wee Nook of Herbals & Oils was located in the back of Jim Tucker's pharmacy. Jim, her son-in-law through her marriage to Marshall, was at the front counter.

"Morning Tess. How are you this morning?"

"Grand, thanks, Jim. And ye?"

"Good, thanks."

"And how are Penny and the kids? I haven't seen them for a few days. Are the children all settled into their new classes?"

"Yep, so far so good." Jim chuckled, his thumbs up. "But it's hard to believe Sarah is going into grade twelve this year."

"Aye. Ye and Penny must be so proud of her. Such a fine lass she is. Both she and Cherokee will do just grand, I'm sure of it. I'm so glad those two have become the best of friends and as thick as thieves." Tessy laughed.

"They are inseparable, that's for certain. It's so great to see all our kids with such wonderful friends, Emma has Becky and Matt has Brendon and Jason. Can sure make for a full house at times, though." Jim laughed.

"Aye, grand friendships are a true blessing, they are. Well, I'm just in to check on any orders. I won't be but a minute."

"Take your time. Let me know if you need anything."

Tessy squatted on a small stool in one of the last aisles, counting her stock, when the bells above the front door tinkled. Then she heard the familiar voice of her nemesis, Mrs. Chamberlain. Tessy winced at the sound.

"Mr. Tucker, I have come to return this box of chocolates."

"Oh. What seems to be the problem with them?" Jim earnestly inquired.

"They were stale, and I want my money back." Mrs. Chamberlain curtly demanded, sliding the box on to the counter towards Jim.

Jim checked the best before date. "Hmm, the expiry date is still good." Jim opened the box to discover there were only a few chocolates left.

"Mrs. Chamberlain, the box is almost empty. What happened to the missing chocolates?"

"Well, I ate them! That's how I found out they were stale." She huffed.

"If you ate almost the whole box, they couldn't have been that bad."

Mrs. Chamberlain raised her chest most indignantly and glared. "Are you calling me a liar, Mr. Tucker?"

"Of course not, Mrs. Chamberlain. However, I'm afraid with the chocolates almost all gone I cannot give you your money back."

"Then I demand another box of chocolates in exchange."

"Mrs. Chamberlain, all the boxes came in at the same time which means the expiry date will be exactly the same on all of them. I certainly wouldn't want you to experience another such unsettling ordeal." Jim cringed, hoping his sarcasm was somewhat masked.

"Humph!" Mrs. Chamberlain huffed. "So, this is how you treat your customers?"

"All right, then. I suppose I could give you one more box. However, if you choose to take it and find that it is unsatisfactory, for the same reason, I would not be able to exchange it for another one."

"Fine! I'll take one. But I can't say I find your attitude or return policy very adequate!"

Jim disappeared down an aisle and came back with the exact same box of chocolates. He handed it to his least favourite customer with the most amicable smile he could muster.

She snatched the box from him. "Thank you."

Just before she was about to stomp out, Tessy knocked a tin off the shelf. Mrs. Chamberlain turned around to see Tessy step out from behind the back aisle. "Humph—you! I should have known you'd be skulking around. Mr. Tucker, I don't know why you allow this witch to sell her lotions and potions in your store." She turned toward the door and exited in the same arrogant fashion in which she arrived.

Tessy gingerly peeked out from behind the shelving and gave Jim a sympathetic, wide-eyed, teeth clinching expression.

"Let's not even go there!" Jim seethed. "I'll be in my office!" He stormed off to fume in private.

My, my, my! That woman can certainly stir up disarray wherever she lands, thought Tessy, shaking her head. She let out a deep sigh and set back to work.

6
It Takes a Village

As it turned out, Tessy didn't have to wait long for an answer from Rosemary. She and her mother, Rose, would be arriving next Tuesday. That gave Tessy exactly one week to prepare.

"'Tis going to be a busy week, for sure!" She tossed the words at Merlin as he leapt up on the mahogany desk just as Tessy hung up the phone.

Tessy remained at the desk for a while longer making a list of things to be done before next Tuesday. She needed to get the spare rooms all freshened, product made up for the store, buy groceries and prepare and freeze some meals. She had to remove Merlin's massive black tail four times in order to complete her list. When she was done, she took the list with her into the kitchen and popped it under a magnet on the fridge. It would help to keep her on track. She decided she would spend the day making product. She wanted to get caught up with her orders so she could solely concentrate on her guests' arrival.

Tessy disappeared into her little herbal kitchen. She pulled down sacks, jars, and bottles of ingredients off the shelves and placed them on a rolling cart. She wheeled it into the main kitchen and got started. Being surrounded by her herbs and oils always brought her great joy. The smells, the textures, and the tastes each had their own spirit to soothe and heal.

She hummed her favourite songs and did a little dance or two as she mixed and measured. She was pouring the last of the beeswax mix into lip balm tubes when she sensed a presence and looked towards the back door. She heard the dogs make a friendly fuss outside and assumed it was some of the neighbourhood children. She looked up as Sage burst through the door. Sage stood wide-eyed and silent; her mouth open.

"Sage, dear! What is it?" Tessy exclaimed. She moved towards the girl just as Tommy entered the kitchen.

"Oh, hello, Tommy. Please come. Sit you two." She motioned them towards the kitchen table. "Excuse the mess."

Sage blankly plunked herself down on the closest chair. "We had the ultrasound done yesterday and everything was just fine. Then we got called back in to see Dr. Kyle again today. He thought he saw something on the ultrasound and wanted me to have another one."

"And?" Tessy beckoned.

"We're having twins!" Sage blurted.

"Oh that, I mean, aye, dear. I know. Congratulations."

"You knew?" Both Sage and Tommy gaped at Tessy. "So, when you mentioned, babies that day, you already knew?"

"Well, I was pretty sure." Tessy chuckled. "I had a premonition a long while ago. I wasn't going to say anything to ye until the doctor confirmed it. I don't mean to take the wind out of your sails or steal your thunder. But I'm really glad the cat is out of the bag, so to speak. We'll talk about all that in more detail at a later date. Isn't it grand news, though?"

"News, for sure. Not sure how grand. What are we going to do? We don't have the room. It's going to be so expensive. And, ooh, how am I going to tell my mom?" Sage broke into tears of hormonal despair.

Tommy got up from his chair and placed a loving arm around his young wife to console her. "Sage. Babe. It'll be fine, you'll see. We'll manage."

Tessy brought over a box of tissue and set it in front of the sobbing, emotional Sage and sat down beside her. She patted her hand and lovingly assured her. "Sage, love. You just need a day or two to get over the shock and catch your breath. You're not in this alone. You have an amazing young man to stand by you, not to mention all of us. Ye know Marshall and I will do all we can and there's Sarah, Cherokee, all the Tuckers, and Dr. Kyle. We are your village, my dear."

7
The Plan

Within a few days, Sage and Tommy had become accustomed to the initial shock of twins and adjusted to their new reality. It did, however, take a couple of extra days for Sage to call and break the news to her mother. To Sage's great relief and after a significant pause in the conversation, Rosemary took the news quite well.

As difficult as it was, Rosemary managed to hold her secret of the surprise visit. Sage's grandmother, Rose, was just beside herself with excitement when the news of twins was shared. She couldn't wait to see her glowing granddaughter.

By Tuesday morning, Tessy had all her orders filled, her guestrooms and the rest of the house freshened and cleansed. The fridge and freezer were packed with delectables, and she felt quite satisfied with her accomplishments. All she had left to do was pop into the shower and get dressed. The phone rang.

"Good mornin' to ye," she answered.

"Good morning, my sweet lady."

"Aye, Marshall, love. How are ye fairing, dear?"

"Well, slow but sure. I think we're making some progress."

"Grand. Glad to hear it."

"I just wanted to give you a quick call before your company arrives and tell you to have a good time. And I love and miss you."

"Thank ye, love. Aye, I miss you, too. They should be here right quick. I was just about to pop into the shower."

"Well, make sure you say hi to them for me."

"Aye, you can be sure I will. Any idea when you'll be home next, love?"

"Not really. If everything goes as planned and on schedule maybe I could sneak away in about a week or so."

"All right. Well, I'll be praying for all to go well."

"Okay, thanks sweetheart. Well, I'd better let you go and get ready. I love you, Tess."

"I love ye, too. Give my love to Dotty and Bert."

"You bet. They say hi, too. Bye honey."

"Bye, love."

Tessy hung up the phone and sighed. How she missed him. She was thankful that she would be busy with company for the next week. It would certainly help those long days go by.

Rosemary and Rose arrived late afternoon, a little weary, but in good spirits. After hugs and welcomes they got settled into their rooms while Tessy put the kettle on. Rosemary was the first to join Tessy in the kitchen.

"Are ye all settled, then, dear?" Tessy greeted.

"Yes, everything is just as lovely as always. Thanks."

"Do ye think your mam would like to rest a while?"

"Oh gosh, no! She has more energy than I do." Rosemary laughed. "I'm sure she'll be right down."

"I'm right here." Rose piped as she appeared from around the corner, a cat in her arms. "Your calico and I were just getting reacquainted. I remember your black cat is Merlin, but what is this darling's name, again?" She snuggled the purring feline.

"Oh, that 'twould be Cordelia, dear."

"That's it!" Rose buried her nose into Cordelia's sweet face.

"Oh, I hope those two haven't been bothering you up in your room. They know they're not to be in there. Wee rascals, the pair of them."

"Oh, it's fine. I encouraged them in."

"Aye, I do seem to remember ye spoiling them a mite when ye were here for the weddin'," Tessy playfully scolded Rose.

"Guilty!" Rose laughed.

Normally, Tessy would have served guests tea in the parlour. However, after having had Rosemary and Rose stay with her for the wedding, she knew they preferred things less formal and more casual.

Rose relinquished Cordelia to the floor, and they all comfortably sat at the kitchen table. They enjoyed their tea and lemon thyme loaf while catching up. Sage was the topic of choice.

"I can't wait to see my darling granddaughter carrying my beautiful great grandbabies!" Rose gushed.

"Yes, it's hard to believe I'm going to be a grandmother soon. And to twins no less!" Rosemary added.

"Aye. New beginnings, 'tis a miracle, to be sure. Wee babes to be loved and cherished by so many. I've invited them for supper, so you'll not have long to wait to see them."

"Oh lovely! Thank you, Tessy," Rose exclaimed. "So, what's

the plan? Should we hide when they come?"

"Well, truth be told, I'm not sure whether that's a good idea or not. Sage has been pretty emotional and I'm not sure she can take one more surprise."

"Ooh, good point. We don't want to land her in the hospital. How do you think we should go about this, then?"

"Well, I was thinking maybe I'd call Tommy and give him a heads-up and then have Sage close her eyes and tell her we have a big surprise. That way she would be a little prepared."

"I think that sounds pretty good."

"All right, then. I'll call Tommy." Tessy made the quick call to Tommy. With the plan now in motion the ladies set to work on preparing supper.

Tommy did his best to conceal the secret and had Sage at the door right on time. Tessy greeted them in the front foyer.

"Well, welcome! Come on in. Sage, we need you to close your eyes, dear. We've got a grand surprise for ye."

Sage gave Tessy and Tommy a puzzled look before doing as she was told and covered her eyes. "Okay, what's going on, you two?" Sage asked.

"Oh, you'll see in a minute, dear."

Tommy gently guided his wife into the front room. When he spotted Rosemary and Rose he waved and displayed a big, friendly smile.

"Just a bit farther, dear. Okay, stand right here." Tessy placed Sage right in front of her mother and grandmother.

"Okay, open your eyes!"

"Surprise!" Everyone yelled.

Sage couldn't believe her eyes and was speechless for a moment. Her mother stood and gathered her daughter in her arms just as Sage's tears began to flow. Moments later there wasn't a dry eye in the room. Even Tommy wiped a tear or two.

What a joyous evening they had. They talked, laughed, and reminisced until late in the evening.

Tommy was the first to check his watch. "Oh, babe. I hate to break this up but we both have to work in the morning." This prompted everyone else to check the time.

"My stars!" Tessy gasped.

"Oh, Sage, honey!" Rosemary added. "You need to go and get some rest, sweetheart. It's so late. I'm sure you must be tired."

"Well, yes, I am a little. But you and Grandma were travelling all day. You must be exhausted."

"Aye, I think we could all use a good night's sleep," Tessy concluded. "I'm sure we'll see ye tomorrow." Everyone stood and the three women escorted the couple to the door.

After the kids left, Rose and Rosemary said goodnight to Tessy and went up to their rooms. Tessy gathered up the cups from the front room and took them into the kitchen before letting the dogs out. While she waited for them to do their business, she washed up the few things that were in the sink.

She had an odd feeling in the pit of her stomach and had no idea why. She let the dogs in, got a glass of water and headed upstairs. After such a lovely evening this murky cloud that followed her to bed was quite an unwelcomed sensation. She hadn't experienced such feelings since those horrid visions of Agnes while in Ireland.

Tessy did her best to push those visions aside as she performed her bedtime ritual. She clicked off the bedside lamp and climbed under the covers. She tossed and turned before drifting into a deep, hazy darkness. As she slept, the fog drifted and swirled about her. She felt it wrap tighter and tighter around her body until she couldn't breathe. She woke with a start and realized she was tightly wound in the bed sheets. She untangled herself and reached for her water glass. She took a large sip, straightened out her bedding and lay back down with a deep sigh. *Tomorrow I will bring my dream journal back up to my room. 'Tis time to start paying attention to what the Summerland's have to tell me.*

She did some deep breathing and eventually settled into a peaceful sleep.

8
Liam and Maggie Bridge the Gap

Dawn slowly crept through the bedroom window. Tessy awoke feeling surprisingly refreshed. She rolled over to see Merlin sitting at the door intently staring at her. She chuckled, shaking her head. "Well, wee one. I see you've been standin' guard over me. Ye always seem to know when there's a storm a'brewing. Bless your wee heart."

Tessy threw back the covers and sat on the edge of the bed a minute. She stretched and yawned, then grabbed her housecoat and wiggled into her slippers. Before leaving her room, she picked up Merlin to properly thank him for his attentive devotion. When she reached the kitchen, she discovered the dogs still snuggled in their beds looking quite content. They were in no rush to get up.

"Well, look at the pair of ye! A couple of lazy-bones this mornin'." This rustled them enough to stretch out their legs and make some playful growls and grumbles. Tessy laughed as she opened the outside door.

"Come on, now. Out ye go."

She got the coffee brewing and cut up some fruit.

Rosemary entered the kitchen with a bright, "Good morning."

"Mornin' dear," Tessy returned. "How was your sleep?"

"Oh, just lovely, thanks. That bed is so comfy." Rosemary stretched.

"Grand to hear. Coffee is ready. I've not got the cups down yet but ye know where they are. Help yourself."

Rosemary reached into the cupboard and pulled out three cups and poured herself a cup. "Are you ready for a coffee, Tess?"

"Aye, dear, I am. Thanks. I'm 'bout done here." The two sat at the table and chatted while they waited for Rose.

"I was hoping to go through some picture albums, if ye think ye and yer mam might have some time today," Tessy said.

"Of course. I'd love that and I'm sure Mother would, as well. We brought along some old papers and files Mom had done years ago on the Haggerty side of the family."

"Oh, how wonderful!" Tessy exclaimed.

"And, what are we so excited about this morning?" Rose chuckled as she came around the corner.

"Good mornin' to ye, Rose," Tessy greeted.

"Good morning, ladies," Rose returned. "My, I'm going to have to set an alarm clock if I sleep in like this every morning." They all laughed.

"No harm in enjoying a good rest," Tessy added. The ladies collaboratively got breakfast ready like they'd been doing it together for years.

"Mom, Tessy is looking forward to seeing all that information you brought with you. That's what we were talking about when you came in."

"Oh, good. Yes, there's a great deal of history packed in those files. I can pop upstairs and get them after we eat, and we can take a look."

"That would be grand, Rose. Thank ye. And I'll show ye what I have come up with since our last visit."

Tessy was quite relieved Rosemary and Rose sounded as eager as she was to start investigating their matching ancestry. She was hoping to make some real progress while they were here. They had just poured their last cup of coffee when there was a tap at the kitchen door and in walked Sage.

"Well, good morning," The ladies chimed.

"Good morning," returned Sage as she gave each of the women a hug.

"What a nice surprise." Rosemary smiled. "I thought you were working this morning."

"I was but my first appointment cancelled and my next one isn't until 11:30. So I thought I'd come hang out with my favourite girls."

"Wonderful! Can I get ye anything, love? A coffee, tea?" Tessy got up.

"Ummm, no coffee, thanks. Unfortunately, coffee and I are not the best of friends right now."

"Well, that's probably for the best anyway. How 'bout a nice cup-o-tea?"

"Sure, if it's not too much trouble."

"Not at all, love."

The four ladies reminisced and laughed comfortably for quite some time. While they tidied up the kitchen, Sage mentioned

Tessy's story of their distant, but combined ancestors, Liam and Maggie Haggerty.

"Oh, yes. I remember Tessy telling that story on my first visit here," Rosemary stated.

"But that was just the short version." Sage begged Tessy to repeat the whole story to her mom and grandma.

Tessy retold the story with as much splendour and enthusiasm as when Sage first heard it. She shared how the handsome Celtic sea captain wooed the elusive Maggie into hopelessly falling in love and eventually marrying him. But not before having to save her. With a little help of an old Crone, Liam tracked down and rescued Maggie from a ruthless Earl that had kidnapped Maggie. Sage enjoyed the telling of this tale as much today as she did when she first arrived in Ladyslipper and met Tessy.

Rose remained silent until Tessy had finished. She looked at Tessy then Sage and held up her finger. "Wait here. I'll be right back."

She returned with an armful of files. Sage jumped up to help her. A minute later, Rose had files sprawled all over the freshly cleaned table. She shuffled through them. "Here. Here it is." Rose triumphantly held up a file. She handed it to Tessy while Sage and Rosemary peered over her shoulder.

"Is that a file on Liam and Maggie?" Sage gasped wide-eyed.

"Aye, my girl! I believe it is," Tessy answered, just as surprised and wide-eyed.

"Yes," gushed Rose. "As soon as you started telling that story I recalled it. I just couldn't remember exactly how it went. It's been a long time since I've heard it. Some of these notes belonged to my mother and grandmother. They both were very interested in family history.

"Wow! Grandma, why haven't you told us anything about these?"

"Well, dear, I didn't think anyone was interested."

Sage checked her watch. "Rats. I have to get going. Well, if you guys find out any more really cool stuff today, keep me posted!" Sage kissed everyone and left.

Between the files Rose supplied and the research Tessy had done, many things fell into place. By the end of the day, after much probing and investigating, they came up with a likely conclusion. When Sage and Tommy arrived for supper that evening Tessy proceeded to share their findings.

She began her tale once the dishes were cleared. "After rescuing Maggie and on their way back to be married, Liam and Maggie stopped in to thank the Crone. The Crone took to Maggie right away and gifted them the amulet and ring as a wedding gift. The Crone, or call her a Wise Woman if ye like, also knew Maggie was pregnant with twins. The Crone had been a twin, but her twin died at birth, and she had no one to pass them on to. She offered to teach Maggie the ways of the Wise Woman. Maggie and Liam agreed.

Liam did not wholly trust the Earl to keep his word or his distance from his pregnant wife, so he built a cabin a stone's throw from the Crone's little hobbit. He could then safely hide and keep Maggie and the babies safe while he was at sea."

Sage's eyes were as large as saucers. "What about the ring and amulet?" she asked.

"Unfortunately, nobody knows how old the amulet and ring are or where they originated," Tessy added. "It seems they will remain a mystery forever."

The group fell silent for a moment, contemplating the compelling family history they all shared.

"So, my dears," Tessy concluded, "that is the end of our story and the beginnings of our ancestry."

"I wonder where the amulet and ring are today?" Sage pondered.

Tessy smiled at Rose and Rosemary. She got up from the table and stepped over to the dining room hutch and pulled open the drawer. She took out the velvet pouch and caressed it in her hands. This was it. After the long journey on which the amulet and ring had taken her, she was now passing them on to the newest clan member who rightfully possessed them. She turned and smiled at Sage.

"Hold out your hand, dear."

Sage did as she was told. Tessy pulled open the drawstring and turned the pouch upside down into Sage's hand. The amulet and ring slipped into her palm. Sage looked close then stared up at Tessy.

"Aye, dear. 'Tis them."

9
An Entrusted Honour

Rose and Rosemary's remaining visit fairly flew by. The parting was teary and heartfelt with promises of weekly updates on the pregnancy. Grandma Rose insisted on leaving an envelope of cash for Sage and Tommy to make a trip to Ontario soon. She thought it important for Sage to visit her siblings before she was too far along in her pregnancy to travel.

Now that Sage was in possession of the amulet and ring Tessy wanted to intensify her lessons on Celtic heritage and Crafting. The following day, Tessy asked Sage to bring over the amulet and ring and be prepared to spend most of the day with her. Tessy shared all she knew about the heirlooms including the heartbreaking story of Agnes and her parents' horrific car accident. Tessy didn't share that painful experience with many, but Sage was now the keeper of these treasures. Tessy felt it necessary for her to know the whole truth. When Tessy finished, Sage looked at her with tears in her eyes.

"Oh Tessy, I am so sorry. I can't imagine how you felt when you finally found out your parents were murdered. And on your honeymoon of all times."

"Aye. It did put a bit of a damper on it, to be sure, but 'twas good to get it all out in the open. And 'twas nice to have Keenan there with me."

"Yes, I'm sure it was comforting to have him there, too."

"Well, 'tis all in the past now and it's time for new beginnings. Those two wee poppets you're carrying will have nothing but sunshine and laughter in their lives."

"Oh, I sure hope so." Sage looked down at her belly and gave it an affectionate rub.

Tessy and Sage spent the rest of the afternoon working on lotions, teas, foot soaks and rubs for mommy-to-be. Tessy also included some teachings on chants and meditations to help Sage relax and sleep. They had been working intently for a couple of hours when Tessy noticed Sage looked a little peaked.

"All right, love. I think we've had enough for today. Ye go in the other room and put your feet up and I'll make us a nice cup o' tea."

"I'm fine. We can—" Sage started to protest.

"No, away ye go." Tessy took Sage by the shoulders and directed her out the kitchen door. On her way to the front room, Sage grabbed the amulet and ring off the table. She was tenderly inspecting them when Tessy came in with the tea.

"Just think, Tessy," she began, "all the people that have touched and worn these two mysterious pieces of jewellery."

"Aye, love. They are ancient. And, they do have a history, to be sure."

"Yes. And now they are my responsibility. I find it rather daunting."

"Daunting? Why on earth daunting?"

"Well, who am I to be put in charge of these?"

"You, my dear girl, are the rightful owner of these treasures. You are gifted, ye carry twins of Haggerty blood and ye are good and kind right down to your very soul. Before long ye will begin to know and feel the sacred power ye possess. Ye carry and sustain human life within you. Two wee lives thrive and grow from your very being. Is that alone not reason enough for ye to hold the treasure that goes with it?"

"Whoa. I guess when you put it like that," Sage blurted.

"I should say! Now, no more doubts. By the time our wee poppets arrive you'll be well versed in all ye need to know and, in turn, pass on to them."

Sage looked at the ancient pieces and then at Tessy. "I feel quite humbled and very honoured to be entrusted with them."

"That's wonderful, love. 'Tis an honour to proudly represent your clan. Now 'tis time to learn of your heritage and pass it along to your offspring. You have the roots of many Wise Women in your soul and there will be many more to come."

Sage set the treasured items on the coffee table and the two sipped their tea in silence. Tessy knew Sage was internally digesting what she just learned.

Sage broke the silence. "So now what should I do with them?"

"Well, love. First, they must be cleansed from all the other lives they have touched. They must become your own."

"How do I do that?"

"There is a full moon coming up next week. Placing stones and sacred jewellery in a full moon is the best way to cleanse and energize them. Until then, I suggest you hold them one at a time in the palm of your hand. Concentrate on them. How they feel, the energy they produce. Be one with them. Then pour your energy into them. Visualize it like a clear beautiful brook running over them, cleansing every bit. Wait here a minute. I have an idea."

Tessy ran upstairs and retrieved the translated note. She rushed back to Sage and sat beside her. She unfolded the note and skimmed over it. "Aye, here we are. Now, while I read this aloud you hold the amulet between your palms, close your eyes and do as I suggested." Sage did as she was asked. Tessy recited the poem.

The following passage has been handed down for many a century, take heed.

Whoever is blessed with this amulet and ring

To all your affairs their power will bring

Follow the path of crystals, gems, herbals and oils

To keep away all curses, evils and spoils

Learn from the Crone what ye can

All Maidens and Mothers make this your plan

For in this wisdom ye will learn and grow

Discovering which is friend and which to be foe.

Find the Clan named after the herbs,

For they are the protected ones with powerful words.

Blessed Be

They then repeated the process with the ring.

"There, then." Tessy smiled. "That should help until you can set them in the light of the full moon."

Sage looked at the jewellery, then at Tessy. "May I write down that chant before I go? I'd like to memorize it."

"Aye, dear. I think that a fine idea."

They both got up and took their cups into the kitchen. While Sage copied the note, Tessy tidied up. She went to the fridge and took out a prepared shepherd's pie for Sage to take home for supper.

"Oh, thank you, Tessy. You didn't have to do that."

"I know, love. But it's getting on, and with Tommy being at work all day you'll both be a hungry pair by the time ye get home."

Sage got up, folded the note, and put it in her bag along with the amulet and ring. She gave Tessy a big hug and held her tight for a few moments.

"I don't know what I would do without you," she softly breathed. She stood back and lovingly looked at Tessy, then sighed. "I love you."

"Aye. I love ye, too. You've brought me such joy."

"Well, before I start to cry, I better go." Sage chuckled and wiped the corner of her eye. Thanks again for this yummy supper. I know Tommy will be really happy."

"You're very welcome, love." Tessy watched out the window until Sage was gone from sight. "Aye, such grand joy ye bring."

10
A Little Fatherly Advice

Marshall lay on the couch with his leg carefully elevated on a couple of pillows. Tessy rushed in with a bag of ice wrapped in a tea towel.

"Here ye go, love," she said, as she gingerly placed the cold pack on his ankle.

"I can't believe how I could have been so stupid and clumsy. I'm just back from Winnipeg and now this!" Marshall grumbled.

"Not stupid at all, love. It was just an accident. There doesn't seem to be anything broken, just a sprain, 'tis all."

"Oh, I know," he groaned.

Tessy got him comfortable, placing the remote for the TV, his cell phone, and the house phone on the coffee table beside him.

"Now, love, would ye like me to get ye some Tylenol for the pain?"

"Ya, that probably wouldn't hurt, if you don't mind. Thank you."

"Not at all, dear. I'll be right back."

On her way to the kitchen the phone rang.

"I'll get it," Marshall hollered. "Hello," he answered, quite curtly.

"Oh, hi Dad. It's Kyle. Did I catch you at a bad time?"

"Oh, no. Sorry, son. I'm just mad at myself. I stepped on a wrench laying on the shop floor and twisted my ankle."

"Oh Dad! It's not broken, is it?"

"No. Just a sprain."

"Oh, that's too bad. Sorry to hear that. I was calling to see if you were going to be home. I've something I'd like to talk over with you."

"Well, I certainly won't be going too far today." Marshall chortled.

Kyle laughed. "Guess not."

"So sure. When were you thinking of coming by?"

"Is now good?"

"Now's great. Just let yourself in when you get here."

"Okay, see you in a few minutes."

Tessy returned in time to hear the latter part of the conversation. She placed a glass of water and the bottle of Tylenol on the coffee table.

"So, who's on their way over?" she asked.

"Oh, that was Kyle. He wants to talk to me about something."

"How grand. How 'bout I pop off for my walk with the dogs, then. That will leave you two to have a dandy visit."

"I'm sure you could stay and join us."

"No, no, it's fine, love. Ye two don't get to spend much time alone anymore. It will be nice for ye both. When I get back, I'll make up a compress of witch hazel and infused calendula and comfrey oil for that ankle."

"All right, dear. Thanks. Oh, could you make sure the front

door is unlocked?"

"Aye, love." Tessy kissed her husband and left.

While Marshall waited, he thought about how proud he was of the son that followed in his footsteps as a doctor. He and his late wife, Evelyne, were proud of all their kids. They were all healthy, strong, intelligent individuals and as different as night and day. That thought planted a smile on his face. Oh, yes, so different. The last time they had all been together was Marshall and Tessy's wedding.

Penny, his oldest, lived right here in Ladyslipper, married to the town pharmacist, Jim Tucker, and owned her own shoe store. Their three beautiful children, Sarah, Matt, and little Emma were the apples of their grandfather's eye. He was so happy he was able to see them almost every day. Sarah and her best friend, Cherokee, were over often concocting something-or-other with Tessy. Matt and his best friends, Brendon and Jason, came over to help with Brigid. And little Emma and her best friend, Becky, arrived almost daily to spread their sunshine and wonderment. As Tessy would say, yes, he was truly blessed.

His next offspring was Brian, a successful architect living in Switzerland with his lovely wife, Anna, and their two children, Luca and Alina. Marshall hated to only see his other two grandchildren and their parents mostly by Skype. He usually heard from them about every two to three weeks. He was looking forward to, one day, taking Tessy to Switzerland to visit them.

Next was his sweet, odd little gem, Janie. Again, a broad smile beamed across Marshall's face. "Ah, Janie. Where in the world are you today?" He mused out loud. Janie was a geologist who travelled the world digging up rocks and fossils. She didn't have much use for people and was always a bit of a loner, even as a child. He only heard from Janie when she was able to get cell service, or she was near a phone.

Then came the twins. Kyle and Kellie, truly as different as night and day. Kyle always knew he'd be a doctor, like his dad. He finished his internship and headed straight off to Africa with Doctors Without Borders. He didn't care about making big money as some specialist in a city clinic somewhere. He wanted to go where he was truly needed and could make a difference. A year and a half ago, when he came home for Marshall and Tessy's wedding, he met and fell in love with Becky's mom, Susan. He soon gave up Africa and moved to Ladyslipper when he discovered they were looking for a new doctor.

Then there was Kellie, oh, Kellie. Being the baby, so to speak, it was really hard not to spoil her. And spoiled, she was. Her siblings mercilessly teased her about being the drama queen of the family. Her life consisted of the latest fashions, hairstyles, cheerleading, and parties. She became a flight attendant and was very good at it. She showed more responsibility than any of her siblings would have ever imagined from her, even if she was a drama queen. Marshall heard from Kellie on his birthday, usually because one of her siblings reminded her, then only when she needed something or was upset.

"Yes, quite the family." Marshall laughed.

A quick knock at the door broke Marshall's train of thought.

He heard it open.

"Hello, Dad?"

"In living room, Kyle," Marshalled called out.

Kyle stepped into the front room. "Hey. How are you doing, old boy?"

"Oh, good," Marshall smiled as he tried to sit up a bit higher.

"Don't move. Can I get you anything?" Kyle asked as he stood over his father.

"No, no. I'm fine. Thanks. Tessy's got me all fixed up, here. I've got everything I need. There's a beer in the fridge if you'd like one. Help yourself."

"No. I'm good for now, thanks. Maybe later." Kyle smiled as he sat down in one of the wingback chairs by the fireplace.

"Well, it's sure good to see you, son."

"Ya, you too, Dad. Sorry I haven't been by much lately."

The two carried on with some small talk for a bit before Kyle went silent.

"What's on your mind, son?"

"It's Susan," Kyle blurted.

"Susan! What's wrong with Susan?"

"Well, nothing's wrong, per se. It's just that she doesn't seem to want to get married. We've been dating for a year and a half and living together for almost six months."

"Have you two discussed it?"

"Yes. Well, I've tried, lots of times. At first, of course, she needed her divorce finalized. Which was fine. But that was over with eight months ago. Every time I bring up marriage, she changes the subject."

"Well, son, she and little Becky have been through quite an ordeal with her ex-husband, from what I understand."

"I know. And I certainly see why she might be apprehensive, but she knows I would never do anything to hurt her or Becky. I don't want to pressure her but neither one of us is getting any younger. I am so ready to get married, adopt Becky, and have more kids. And, yes, Susan does want, at least, one more child. We have talked about that."

"Have you bought a ring, yet? Or, actually asked her to marry you?"

"Well, no. Not exactly."

"Well, son, I would suggest you drop the subject for a while and give her a little more time. Then, take a trip into the city, pick out a stunning diamond, get down on one knee and romantically propose. What's the worst that can happen? At least then you'd know for sure. You might be pleasantly surprised."

Kyle looked at his dad, displayed a wide, slightly embarrassed grin and shook his head. "Guess I should have thought of that a little sooner, myself. Thanks, Dad. Sounds like a plan. That's exactly what I'm going to do. Think I'll have that beer now. Want one?"

"Well, I took a Tylenol a little while ago but, what the heck. Sure. A beer sounds great."

11
Picturing the Future

October arrived in grand form. The air was crisp and fresh. Harvest was over and all along the fence lines the goldenrod exploded in full display. The leaves turned to vibrant hues of yellow, orange, and red while the glorious smells of autumn wafted through the air.

As far as Tessy was concerned, life was as grand as it could get. Marshall's ankle had healed nicely, and he was back to tinkering with Brigid. Sage and Tommy decided to take that surprise visit down east to spend some time with Sage's older brother, Rowan, and her younger sister, Saffron.

Sarah and Cherokee were sitting at Tessy's kitchen table with their binders and textbooks sprawled before them. Sarah flipped her binder closed and let out a frustrated huff.

Cherokee glanced up from her papers. "What's the matter?"

"Oh, I just can't think of a project for our English assignment," she grumbled.

Tessy was mixing up cookie dough while the girls studied. She turned and gave Sarah a sympathetic look.

"Well dear, what is it you're to be working on?" Tessy enquired as she walked over to the table. The teacher within Tessy was never far.

"Something about future goals and ambitions. I mean, how

do you really know what those might be. I have ideas about stuff I want to do but how do you explain that without it looking like a dreamy wish list? Have you started anything yet, Cherokee?"

"No. I'm having a little trouble with that myself." Cherokee sighed.

"Well, now." Tessy pulled out a chair to sit down. "Ye girls both showed an interest in alternative healing. Are ye still thinking of proceeding with that?"

"Yes." They both chimed.

"But," Sarah said. "Neither of us can pinpoint exactly what area we want to go into."

"Well, who says you have to pinpoint anything down right now. I think that would be the whole point of this assignment. To help ye focus on the areas that interest ye most."

"Hmmm, I guess." Sarah was deep in thought.

"Is there any rule that the two of ye can't do a similar project?" Tessy absently asked. She rose and moved back to her cookie dough.

Sarah and Cherokee looked at one another. "No. I don't think so. Why?" Cherokee shook her head.

"When is the project due?" Tessy asked.

"Not until April. It will be a big percentage of our passing grade, though." Sarah winced.

"Well, I've an idea that might help ye along."

"Great! What?" both girls asked excitedly.

Tessy chuckled. "Have ye heard of a vision board or journal?"

"Is that where you cut pictures and stuff out of magazines?"

Sarah asked.

"Aye, that along with other things."

"Hey." Sarah brightened. "That sounds kinda' cool. What do you think Cherokee?"

"I love it!" Cherokee's smile lit up her face.

"Awesome!" Sarah squealed. "Thanks for the idea, Tessy!" She rushed over and gave Tessy a hug.

Tessy laughed. "You're very welcome, my dears. Now, when you're ready to get started I've a few boxes of magazines up in the attic you're welcome to. I was just thinking the other day of bundling them up and taking them to the recycling station. This will save me the trip; at least, for now."

The girls were ecstatic. With their mental load lightened, they closed their books and helped Tessy finish with her cookies. Soon the kitchen smelled sweet and cinnamony with warm and chewy oatmeal chocolate chip cookies. The girls sat and savoured one each and talked about their new project.

"Sarah, are you going to do a vision board or journal?" Cherokee asked between bites.

"Hmmm, not sure. I was thinking journal. You?"

"Yep, me too."

"Lovely. Well, ye girls are more than welcome to come over here and work on them anytime ye like. We can go on up to the attic right now and I can show ye where the boxes are." Tessy offered.

"That would be great," Cherokee said. "Let's go. I love going up in your attic, Tessy. It's magickal and filled with the most interesting things."

"I find it a little bit scary," Sarah added. "Well, maybe eerie is a better word."

"Really?" Cherokee scrunched up her face at her friend.

The girls followed Tessy up the main stairs, down the hall, and to the little door heading up into the mysterious large space. The stairs creaked and musty smells tickled their noses. The oval stained-glass windows cast multi-coloured rays throughout the room and highlighted the dancing dust particles. For a storage area it was really quite organized. Tessy made sure of that. All the Christmas ornaments here, Easter there, and Halloween over there. Not to mention all the other storage items an attic can collect. To get to where they were going they passed trunks, old bikes, photographs, and furniture. They were headed over to the darkest corner of the room.

"I'm pretty sure they're over this way," Tessy said, more to herself than the girls. She pulled a dangling string and a light popped on with a click. "Ahh. There ye are. Hiding in the corner, are ye?" Tessy chuckled seeming proud to have found them so quickly. "Ye girls should find lots of information in these. There are magazines filled with gardening, herbal, health, nature pictures, and articles."

The girls stared at a number of boxes filled to the brim with magazines. Cherokee reached to the closest box and pulled out a small stack. A very large spider dangled down from the magazines. Sarah spotted it first and let out a sudden screech. The spider dropped to the floor and scurried under a nearby trunk.

"Eeew! I hate spiders!" Sarah shuddered and flapped her hands about.

"They won't harm ye, dear," Tessy assured her. "Spiders are timid wee creatures and wish you no ill will."

"Yah, Sarah. Tessy taught me all about spiders. They are actually really amazing once you get past the look of them. Let's see if I can remember." Cherokee squinted at Tessy. "They weave the pattern of life. They teach us that what we weave now we will experience in the future. They represent, umm, creativity, fate and divine feminine energy."

Tessy beamed. "Aye, very well done, my dear! And, if ye have spiders you'll not have any other bugs in your house, to be sure."

"Yuck. Seriously, I have to start liking spiders now?" Sarah groaned.

"Yep. It should be easy hanging around up here. You'll see. In just a few short weeks you'll have them all named," Cherokee teased.

Sarah shuddered again and gave her friend a playful sneer but remained silent. Each magazine she picked up after that was well inspected before she carted a small stack downstairs.

Before long, the kitchen table was covered in magazines. The girls thumbed through the lovely pictures but weren't really sure what they were looking for.

"So, how does this work, Tessy?" Sarah asked. "Do we have to pick out certain things that go with what we think we want to write about?"

Tessy handed each of the girls a pair of scissors. "Well, that might be a way to go about it. I would suggest ye just start cutting out pictures that really speak to ye. And, not just pictures, but words or phrases that jump out at ye."

"That sounds pretty easy," Cherokee chirped.

"Yes, too easy. No offence, Tessy, but that doesn't really sound like our goals and ambitions."

Tessy chuckled. "Oh, my dears. You'd be surprised what can be channelled to ye when ye get out of your own way. Start noticing words and phrases that just pop out at ye. Make sure ye concentrate on the positive. The ones that make ye tingle and smile."

The girls looked at one another but said nothing and cut out pictures, words, and phrases. Before long each girl had an impressive pile of clippings in front of her.

Tessy disappeared upstairs for a few minutes and came back down with a well-worn scrapbook. She paused reverently looking at it, then placed it on the table between the girls. "I've not looked at this in a very long while." Tessy smiled. "This is my vision journal that I put together many years ago. Funny, looking in it now makes me realize just how many of my visions have come to fruition."

The girls stopped what they were doing and pulled their chairs close. Cherokee gingerly opened the cover. It was stiff and crumpled from the effects of hardened glue and age. The pages inside were slightly yellowed and stiff but they were filled with inspiring pictures, words and messages. It was like seeing Tessy through a magnifying glass or peering into her private diary. They looked at one another then up at Tessy.

"Are you sure you want us to see this?" Cherokee asked.

"Aye, dear. 'Tis fine. Go on ahead. 'Twill give ye a good idea of where to start."

12
Full Moon Rising

Marshall watched his Irish bride scurry about the kitchen while he enjoyed his mid-morning coffee. He had been out in the Quonset working on Brigid.

"What are you so busy at, darling?" he finally asked.

"Oh! 'Tis the full moon tonight."

"Ahhh, the full moon." He didn't need any more of an explanation. He had been married to this beautiful enchantress long enough to know the importance of *her* full moons.

"Aye, and not just any full moon. The Hunter's Moon." She looked aghast at him like he should know. She softened her expression and smiled. "'Tis an important moon. It represents new goals, protection, spirituality, and resolution. It's also called the Blood Moon, but I prefer Hunter's Moon."

"Honey, all your moons are important to you." Marshall got up, put his cup in the dishwasher and pecked his wife on the cheek. "Have fun." He winked as he walked out the door and back to his other love, Brigid.

Tessy needed some spring water to charge in the moonlight. Since there were no springs close by, the next best thing was rainwater from her barrels. She'd remembered to scoop out a couple of jars before they emptied them for the season. She would use the sacred Moon Water to enhance divination, meditations, elixirs, and spirit work.

Next, she wandered about the house with a basket gathering an array of crystals and stones to be re-charged for the coming month. In her bedroom, she sorted through her favourite pieces of jewellery. She wanted to be sure the gems would be empowered and ready to wear. Full moons were a big deal at Ashling Manor.

The phone rang. She walked over to her bedside table to answer it. She was excited to see the name that flashed up.

"Sage, love!" she exclaimed. "You're home!"

"Hi, Tess. Yes."

"How was your visit, dear? When did ye get home?"

"The visit was wonderful. And we got home late last night."

"Grand, dear. How are ye feeling?"

"Pretty good. It was great to see everyone, but boy, they sure kept us busy. I'm a little tired and, truthfully, it's really nice to be home."

"Aye, love. And it's grand to have ye home. Oh, before I forget, tonight is the full moon. You'll need to place the amulet and ring in full moonlight to cleanse them."

"Oh, okay. Thanks. I would have forgot, for sure. Well, Tommy is calling me so guess I'd better go for now. I promise to come over soon. Bye."

"Bye, love. Make sure to get some rest."

"You bet. Thanks. Bye."

Tessy was so happy to have Sage and Tommy back safe and sound. She now felt quite satisfied that everything was set and ready for the evening. Tessy spent the rest of the day preparing product. She relished in knowing every lotion, potion, salve, and balm were much more potent in the realm of a full moon.

Both Marshall and Tessy stopped for lunch but resumed their tasks shortly after. It was late afternoon when Marshall re-appeared. Tessy was clearing up the kitchen. Marshall had grease smeared on his face, his coveralls were stained, and his hands were unrecognizable. He lunged towards Tessy, pretending he wanted a kiss.

"Not in your life, ye dirty scoundrel. Way off ye go to the shower before ye come near me." Tessy smirked.

"Okay but have a beer ready for me when I get back." Marshall requested as he walked down the hall. "Please and thank you," he yelled on his way up the stairs. He descended back down, shortly after, wet-haired and a new man.

"Ahh, that feels better," he exhaled as he wrapped his arms around Tessy. They kissed.

"Aye! Ye smell a mite better, too!" Tessy teased as she handed him his beer. "Ye know, if you're going to continue to be coming in the house and dirtying up my bathroom like this, maybe we ought to consider putting a shower in the bathroom Quonset."

"Hey! That might not be a bad idea. It's all plumbed in out there. However, I really don't want to discuss any more plumbing problems after what I've recently been through in Winnipeg." Marshall took a long sip of his beer. Tessy chuckled as she poured herself a glass of wine.

That night, while most of the world slept, the full Hunter's Moon shone with all its glory. It filled the Earth with energy and pulled at the great tides of the oceans. All was as it should be until the first breaking rays of light shimmered and woke the early morning prowlers.

13
Henry!

Marshall got up from the breakfast table, grabbed the coffee pot and poured the remains into their cups. "So sweetheart, were you serious about putting a shower in the Quonset bathroom?"

"Aye. Don't you think it's a fine idea?"

"I think it's a brilliant idea. I don't know why we didn't think of it sooner. I'll give the guys a call today and see what they say. I'm pretty sure all we'll need to do is install one of those shower kits."

"That sounds grand, love. Well, looks like you're not quite done with plumbing renovations just yet." She chuckled.

Marshall groaned before taking a sip of coffee.

They each went about their day. Marshall headed out to the shop bathroom to design and measure. Tessy decided to re-arrange her herbal kitchen. The phone rang. Tessy answered the wall phone hanging just outside the herbal kitchen door.

"Good mornin' to ye," she gaily greeted.

"Tessy, it's Sage. It's gone!" she howled. "I've lost it!"

"Sage, dear. What's wrong? Lost what?"

"The amulet. It's gone!"

"Gone? What do ye mean gone? What happened to it?"

"I don't know. I did as you said and put it and the ring out in the moonlight. I put them on a tray and now the amulet is gone!"

"Where did ye put the tray?"

"Outside, on the balcony table. That was the only place the moonlight was really shining. I went out to check them this morning and that's when I noticed it missing. Oh, Tessy! What am I going to do?"

"So, they were outside on the balcony for the night?"

"Yes."

"Was it light out when you went to check them?" Tessy asked.

"Yes, I forgot all about them until just now."

There was a moment of silence then Tessy growled. "Henry!"

"Henry? Who's Henry?"

"Oh, Henry is a dear friend of mine. We've known each other for years."

"So, a friend of yours by the name of Henry somehow climbed up to our balcony in the middle of the night and stole the amulet?"

"Not exactly, dear. I'll be right over. I'll explain then."

Tessy grabbed the car keys, ran out to the shop and yelled in the door, "Popping over to Sage's, love. Shan't be long." She jumped in the car and arrived on Sage's doorstep in record time. She ran up the stairs to their flat and knocked.

Sage pulled open the door. "That was fast."

"Aye. Now, let's go out on your balcony and see what we can see."

"Well, I cannot see how anyone could possibly get up to this balcony without an extremely long ladder. And who is Henry?"

70

Tessy stood out on the deck and surveyed the surroundings. It was exactly as she suspected. "Aye, there ye are. Ye little beggar."

Sage looked toward the large tree Tessy was addressing. "Are you talking to that huge crow over there?"

"'Tis not a crow, 'tis a raven. And, aye, 'tis Henry."

"That's Henry?"

"Aye. And 'tis a good thing ye checked outside when ye did or the ring 'twould be gone, as well." Tessy moved over to the railing closest to the tree. "Henry!" she barked. "What have ye done with the shiny trinket? Ye go fetch it straight off and bring it back."

Henry looked right at Tessy and cocked his head. He threw his beak high into the air and began to cackle, mercilessly taunting her.

"Oh, ye sassy wee beggar!" Tessy huffed and moved into the apartment. This wasn't the first time she and Henry had been down this path. She needed a minute to think. She asked Sage for the tray the amulet and ring had been on. She went back out. Henry was silent, patiently waiting for Tessy's return. She placed the tray on the table and tapped it.

"Henry, ye bring the shiny trinket back that was on this tray and I'll have a nice, hard-boiled egg for ye at home."

Henry remained perched and quiet, as if thinking. The standoff between the two lasted a good while. Tessy finally called, "Uncle," and went into the apartment.

Sage finally spoke. "So, what's up with you and Henry?"

"Well, Henry has lived in the trees behind Ashling Manor

for years. He loves to tease and torment the dogs to exhaustion, but we've all become like family. He joins us on our rambles and he and I have had many a grand chat. Ravens mate for life and he had a lovely dear I named Harriet. One day, a few years ago, she never returned. I'm afraid she was shot. It was about the same time I lost Dermot. We spent many a day consoling one another. He stays most winters and I feed him. And, in return, he brings me shiny objects like bottle caps, sparkly rocks, coins and paper clips. I've quite a collection. Ravens bring protection and new beginnings. They are very smart and quite loyal. They can even mimic people as well, if not better, than parrots. I really can't imagine Ashling Manor without him."

As heartbroken as Sage was, there was little more to be done. Tessy declared defeat, for today, and went home. She kept her promise to Henry and left his favourite treat, a hard-boiled egg for him. Three days later Tessy stepped out onto her back step and there was the amulet. She scanned the yard. Henry was sitting on the clothesline post staring at her.

"Well now, Henry. Thank ye kindly for returning the amulet. Ye really are a smart wee scamp, ye are." Tessy went back into the kitchen. She returned with a special treat. The riff between the two was patched and their friendship soon returned to their mutual and unconditional respect.

14
Murder at Ashling Manor

When the Wheel of the Year turns to October, Tessy's attention always turns to Samhain. She spends a great deal of the month planning, decorating, and preparing for this most special day of the year. Her Halloween festivities always include her friends, neighbours and, well basically, the whole town. She delights in having her grandchildren and their friends help with the yard decorations. There are plenty of pumpkins to carve, scarecrows to dress and ghosts to set into motion. October is a busy time at Ashling Manor.

It's also a time to remember and honour dear departed loved ones. Mid-month, Tessy will set up a special altar with photographs and keepsakes of ancestors, family and friends who have passed. She finds this a difficult time, as strong feelings for Dermot pop up. Marshall is extremely, understanding, as he too, remembers his departed Evelyne fondly.

There is another special tradition Tessy holds dear. She narrates a scary story for the different age groups of children that visit on Halloween night. With each age group the story gets a little scarier. This year, for the wee ones and pre-teens, it would remain much the same. She did, however, have something quite different in mind for the teenagers.

* * *

At the end of August, Tessy invited Sarah, Cherokee, Matt, and six of their friends over for a wiener roast to discuss her idea. She wondered, instead of their scary story, if they might be interested in a Murder Mystery Halloween night at Ashling Manor. The kids were crazy for the suggestion and couldn't wait.

Tessy set to work on her plan. This gave her enough time to write a fairly simple murder mystery that would take approximately a couple of hours to play out and get solved. She included characters for each person attending. It had been quite an undertaking but one she enjoyed immensely. She didn't want to limit the kids on their costumes, so she set the scene as a Halloween party.

By mid-September, Tessy had the story written. Before she mailed out the storyline, character description cards and nametags to the kids, she decided to run it by Marshall to see what he thought.

"Won't that give me the advantage of knowing who the killer is?" Marshall grinned.

"Nye. Nobody will know who the killer is until that night. That way no one can spill the beans."

"How did you manage that?"

Tessy just smiled and winked. "Now, bear with me, as most of this is in point form." She began, "A Murder at Ashling Manor.

The victim is a beautiful, orphaned female named Beverly.

She's a university student in fashion design.

She's about to turn twenty-one and will soon be the sole

beneficiary to a very large inheritance.

She's a popular, flirtatious cheerleader, and has a part-time job at an up-and-coming, fashion company.

She lives with her legal guardian, Rebecca May, who has been her nanny since childbirth. Her lazy, shady, Uncle Martin, lives with them.

Beverly informs Rebecca May that she wishes to have a combination Halloween/birthday party.

The arrangements are made, and the invitations sent out."

Tessy stopped and looked up at Marshall. He said nothing but raised his eyebrows and nodded.

"Okay," Tessy continued. "Next are the character descriptions and their relationship to the victim. These are the cards I'm sending out to everyone. I'll give you yours, as well. Again, in point form."

"Who I am?" Marshall asked.

"You'll see, soon enough." Tessy chuckled.

"Amy: played by Sarah

- A medical student.
- Beverly's best friend. They have been best friends since childhood.
- Amy can't believe anyone as popular and beautiful could possibly be her friend.
- Amy believes that this will soon come to an end when Bev graduates, comes into lots of money, and becomes a famous fashion designer.

"Ginni: played by Cherokee
- Also a childhood friend.
- She and Bev have always had a relationship filled with turmoil.
- Ginni has just as strong personality as Bev, although they are as different as day and night.
- Ginni is a gifted herbalist and close friends with Amy, as well.
- Affectionately, nicknamed Herbie.

"Ryan: played by Brendon
- Bev's current boyfriend.
- Presently suffering with an eye infection.
- Law student and star athlete (AKA The Rocket).
- Can't stand her flirting with other guys.
- He feels Bev is growing tired of him and will drop him soon.
- He has been secretly seeing Misty.

"Misty: played by Jodi
- Also very popular and on the cheerleading squad.
- Studying the Arts
- She and Bev are rivals in almost everything they do.
- Misty is extremely jealous of Bev's relationship with Ryan as she wants him for herself.

"Samantha: played by Shelley

- Co-worker at the fashion company.
- Believes she is a much better fashion designer but is getting overlooked because of Bev.
- A major promotion lies in the balance.

"Grace: played by Teresa
- The odd duck of the group.
- Medical student.
- Works part time at the nearby pharmacy.
- Quiet, not very trusting and a little strange.
- Always had to work hard for everything.
- Secretly believes everyone in the group is pretentious.

"Brad: played by Jonathon
- An ex-boyfriend of Bev's whom she still flirts with.
- She is considering taking him back, but he doesn't know.
- Tired of her games.
- Brad is a law student.

"Jerry: played by Jason
- Is also an ex-boyfriend Bev likes to toy with.
- Jerry is a medical student struggling financially to stay in university.
- Good friends with Brad.
- Is jealous and intimidated by Ryan.
- Is a little clumsy and sometimes teased as Jerry Jughead.

"Uncle Martin, played by you, Marshall." Tessy looked up at her husband.

"Oh, great! Shady old Uncle Martin!" Marshall playfully threw up his arms.

Tessy laughed and continued.

"Uncle Martin: played by Marshall
- Bev's Uncle Martin believes he should have inherited his brother's estate and guardianship over his niece.
- He has been living at the estate on a small allowance.
- He also believes he would inherit everything should something happen to Beverly.

"Rebecca May: played by me
- Beverly's nanny since birth.
- Firm but kind.
- Believes she will be cast aside once Bev takes over, as there will be no longer any need for her.

"Inspector Crawford: played by Matt
- Very thorough.
- Looks at all the evidence and takes into account everyone's motives and alibis."

Tessy looked up at Marshall who had been intently listening. "Well, any ideas as to who the murderer is, yet?"

"Not a clue. Everyone seems to have a bit of a motive. Who

is playing Beverly, by the way?"

"Nobody. It wouldn't be much fun for someone to play dead all evening. She has been murdered before anyone arrives. You'll see as we go along."

"That's brilliant!"

"Why, thank ye, love."

Tessy was relieved to hear she hadn't given too much information away on the storyline and character description cards. She mailed them out the third week in September. This would give everyone plenty of time to work on his or her character. She also included a personalized note to each guest. She wanted to assure them their character had nothing to do with their own personality. She added, when they arrive at Ashling Manor there would be cue cards and props provided.

The kids came over every day after school for the week prior to Halloween. They were so excited about the Murder Mystery and acted non-stop. They practised in character as they decorated and helped out. By the time October 31st rolled around, the yard and Ashling Manor were adorned in all the grand ghoulish elegance expected. And the actors had their characters down pat.

Unfortunately, Mother Nature did not cooperate as much as she could have. The day was cool, along with scattered snow flurries. Mid-afternoon, Tessy peeked out the kitchen window. "Oh, poor wee tykes. 'Tis not going to be the nicest of evenings for trick-o'-treating."

15
Who Dun It?

The early part of Halloween evening went as planned. Tessy and Marshall welcomed all their costume-clad guests. Every fairy, pirate, princess, vampire, and witch were received and entertained. Each child excitedly accepted their scary story along with a bag of goodies before continuing on their way.

The evening became extremely blustery. This made for a very quiet Samhain at Ashling Manor. Time drew near for the murder to take place. Tessy was a little concerned as to whether the cast would show up.

"Oh, I don't know what I was thinking." Tessy started to doubt her idea.

"Stop fretting, darling. Everyone will be here."

"Aye, yer right, love. The storm actually sets the perfect mood for a murder." Tessy concurred. She felt reassured that the evening would play out as planned.

Time ticked on and then the doorbell finally rang. Tessy gave Marshall a look of positive anticipation and took a deep breath. She gave the side table she had placed at the door a quick glance to make sure all the cue cards and props were in order. She grabbed the door handle.

"Action," she called out.

Within fifteen minutes every cast member showed up in

costume and in character. As each person entered, Tessy handed them their cue cards to study.

Rebecca May ushered them between the parlour and the dining room so everyone was comfortable mingling and moving about. She informed them Beverly had not been feeling well earlier in the day but promised she'd be down in due course. Twenty-minutes passed and still no sign of Beverly.

As instructed on her cue card, Amy, being Bev's best friend, decided she would go upstairs to see what was taking her so long. It took a few minutes, longer than it should have. Then there was a blood-curdling scream. The crowd froze.

"Everyone, into the parlour," Uncle Martin ordered. "Stay here."

As on cue, the boys refused to listen. They and Rebecca May followed him up the stairs. They found Amy standing outside Beverly's bedroom door with her hands over her face and shaking. They looked in and there was a fictitious Beverly on the bed with a knife in her chest.

"Brad, isn't that your army knife?" Ryan blurted.

The fun was about to begin! Tessy was exhilarated.

They returned to the parlour and informed the girls of their gruesome find. Amy was escorted to the couch to lie down. Rebecca May called the police. Shortly, thereafter, Inspector Crawford appeared at the door. (Matt had been there the whole time in another costume then quickly changed).

Rebecca May explained the incident on the way into the parlour. The inspector listened intently then scanned the room of likely suspects.

"I would like to see the body," he said, then added, "nobody leaves." He glared at everyone before exiting the room. Rebecca May led him up the stairs, down the hall, and to the bedroom door.

"Please remain outside," he ordered. "Has anyone disturbed the body?"

"Martin checked to see if he could find a pulse," Rebecca said.

"Did he touch anything else?"

"Not that I know of. You can ask him when you go back downstairs."

Tessy was thrilled with Matt's performance.

Inspector Crawford remained upstairs for a few minutes longer pretending to look at the corpse. While investigating the crime scene he paid special attention to the prescription bottle and almost empty teacup on the bedside table. He soon joined Rebecca May in the hallway and suggested they return to the parlour to question her guests.

They stepped into the room just in time to hear Uncle Martin state, "Well, he honestly can't think one of us had anything to do with her murder."

"Oh, but I can," Inspector Crawford assured, as he surveyed the room. "I won't know for sure until I have questioned you all individually." He took out his notebook and copied down everyone's name.

"So, Martin, let's start with you. If you will follow me."

Martin glanced around looking as nervous as a cat in a room full of rocking chairs. The two disappeared into the dining room.

One by one, they each took their turn being questioned in the other room by the inspector. Everyone stayed on cue and soon the parlour was filled with likely suspects. Inspector Crawford remained quiet for a long while, reviewing his notes, deep in thought.

He began, "Now that I have questioned you individually, I would like to ask you a few questions as a group." The suspects all glanced around at one another, each suspecting the other.

"Amy. I understand you found the body."

"Y, y, yes," she stammered.

"According to what I have in my notes, the other guests said you were gone an exceptionally long time before they heard you scream. Can you explain what you were doing during that time?"

Amy looked around the room. "Ummm," she hesitated. "Oh, I went to the bathroom before I went to check on Bev." She conveyed an air of relief.

"Did anyone see you?" The inspector looked up from his notes.

"Of course not!" Amy blurted.

"Hmmm." The inspector tapped his pen on the notebook.

"Ryan, just before she was running out on some errands, Rebecca May said you came over to see Bev earlier this afternoon. Is that true?"

"Yes, sir." Ryan rubbed his sore eye as noted on his character card. "I knew she wasn't feeling too well and wanted to see how she was doing? I made her a cup of tea and sat with her for a while."

"How was she when you left her?"

"She was feeling much better. She said she wanted to take a nap, so I left."

"Hmmm." The inspector scratched his head and looked over to Ginni.

"Ginni. You're an herbalist. Is that correct?"

"Yes."

"It's been stated you and Bev are known to exchange hostile words from time to time."

"Ya, I guess. That doesn't mean I wanted her dead."

"Have you had such a conversation within, say, the last couple of days?" The inspector moved a little closer to her.

"No, not at all. I haven't even seen her this week."

"So, you haven't given her any herbs in the last few days?"

"No. None."

"Grace. Rebecca May stated that you made a prescription delivery here for Bev earlier in the day. Is that true?"

"Yes. Bev called me this afternoon and asked me if I would drop off her diabetic medication. Oh, and I heard Ryan in the background ask to throw in some Visine. Like I haven't got better things to do than be their little errand girl!"

"But you did drop the delivery off? Correct?" The inspector repeated.

"Yes, I had to make another delivery not far from here, so I dropped it off in the mailbox."

"Where were you when you heard Amy scream?"

"I was in the dining room with Ginni when Samantha ran in."

"Samantha, you were a co-worker of Bev's, were you not?"

"Yes."

"And, why were you running into the dining room? Where were you just before that?"

"I walked down the hall and headed to the kitchen, but I stopped when I got to the door."

"And, why was that?"

Samantha glanced towards Misty then Ryan. "I saw Ryan and Misty in the kitchen kissing." The room filled with gasps and whispers. "I didn't want them to see me, so I ran back into the dining room." Samantha lowered her head.

"Hmmm." The inspector turned toward Misty and Ryan. "Is this true?"

Misty stepped closer to Ryan and put her hand on his chest. "Yes!" she cried. "It's true! We're in love!"

Ryan quickly removed her hand. "I don't know what she's talking about. It, it, it just happened. I didn't mean for it to happen."

Misty stared at Ryan. "What do you mean, just happened? How can you say that?"

"Enough!" the inspector yelled. "I'll get back to you two in a minute. Brad. Ryan asked if that was your knife upstairs? Is it in fact yours?"

"I, I, I'm not exactly sure. It looks like my army knife, but it went missing a few days ago."

"Missing! What do you mean missing?" the inspector asked.

"I noticed it gone from my drawer about three or four days ago."

"And how would it go missing? Who would be likely to take it?"

"I don't know." Brad thought for a moment, then glanced over at Jerry. "You're the only one who has been in my room in the last week."

"Me!" Jerry looked like he was going to be sick. Then he cracked. "Yes. Okay, I took it, but I didn't kill her. I received a letter saying all I had to do was steal your knife and put it in an envelope marked T.R. I was to leave it at the campus office and pick up an envelope with my name on it with $250 bucks in it. Brad, you know I need the money."

Brad gave Jerry a disgusted look. "You, son of a b—"

"Brad, I didn't know this was going to happen, honest. I'm sorry, man."

"And, you have no idea who T.R. is?" asked the inspector.

"No. None. Honest!"

Everyone remained quiet for a few minutes.

Uncle Martin broke the silence. "Well, Inspector. No one here has those initials, so I guess we're all free to go?"

The inspector took a long look at Uncle Martin, then scanned the room once again. (Matt took a look at his last cue card and smiled before going back into character).

"Ryan, I believe you have a nickname, do you not?"

Ryan started to fidget. "Yah, so?" He moved closer to the edge of his seat.

"And what is that nickname?"

Ryan looked around the room at everyone staring at him.

"Ryan. Answer the question," the inspector barked.

The rest of the room put it together and all chimed. "The Rocket!"

Ryan got up to run but was tackled and held down by Brad and Jerry.

"Why did you do it Ryan?" Amy cried. "How did you do it?"

Ryan stood and dusted himself off with a free hand while Brad and Jerry stayed close by.

"Okay! Yes, I came over earlier today. Both Rebecca May and Martin were out. We fought. I knew she was going to dump me and go back to Brad. I calmed her down and said I'd make her a cup of tea. I put some Nightshade in the tea as well as some Visine just to make sure. It didn't take long after that. I put her to bed, and before I left, I wrote a note to Rebecca May that Bev was asleep and not to wake her."

Ginni stood up and blurted, "So that's why you were asking me all those questions about poisonous plants. It had nothing to do with a law paper that was due!"

"No, Herbie, there was no paper." Ryan lowered his head.

"So, what's up with the Visine in her tea?" Brad asked.

Grace provided the answer. "Visine has tetrahydrozoline in it which shrinks blood vessels. High levels can be fatal. Side effects are low body temperature and blue fingernails and lips."

"Very good, Grace." The inspector congratulated her, then continued, "So, Ryan, you knew Rebecca May and Martin would suspect you immediately and that is why you also used the knife. She was already dead. I knew she had been poisoned. Her fingernails and lips were blue and there was very little blood around the knife wound."

"I wasn't positive she was dead and so I thought I'd use Brad's knife to frame him for the murder." He threw Jerry an angry glare. "It probably would have worked, too, if Jughead had just kept his big trap shut! I snuck upstairs while everyone was wandering around and planted the knife."

Misty cried bitter tears. "But if you broke up with her we could have been together."

"Sorry, Misty. Bev was coming into millions. How could I just walk away from that? If I couldn't have her and her millions, nobody could."

Everyone looked around and then clapped and cheered. Tessy was thrilled with all the great performances.

"Bravo!" she exclaimed. "Wonderful job!"

"That was awesome." Cherokee agreed. "Matt, you nailed the inspector roll."

"Thanks Cher. It was a blast."

Tessy made sure everyone had refreshments and they all gathered in the front room.

"Great murder mystery, Tessy." Sarah held up her glass. "To Tessy." Everyone toasted.

"Thank ye, my dears. It was grand fun putting it together."

"Hey?" Matt piped. "Who ended up with the millions? Uncle Martin?"

Tessy laughed. "Ahh, nye. There was a clause in the will stating if something should happen to Beverly that Rebecca May would inherit everything. Well, except for a small fishing cabin in northern Manitoba and a monthly allowance that went to Uncle Martin."

Matt slapped his grandfather on the back. "Tough luck, old boy."

Everyone laughed.

16
Pragmatic Precautions

The vivid hues of October turned to the grey, dismal days of pre-winter. Leafless trees displayed their true shape and form while showing off their winterberries and cones. The days grew shorter, and temperatures dropped. Ladyslipper was ready for winter's deep sleep.

With Samhain over and Sage and Tommy safely settled for the coming winter, life was restored to its sweet, mundane normality. Further renovations at the Doctor's Inn required Marshall's attention and Tessy found herself on her own once again. She felt a little melancholy.

She sat at the kitchen table making out her Christmas card list. She had to start early to ensure the ones heading over to Ireland made it in good time. She missed her twin brother Keenan, her homeland and all the family that resided there. She looked up from her list and gazed out the window. Besides missing her family, Tessy assumed her mood had something to do with her lack of sleep. She'd had another one of those disturbing dreams last night.

They still weren't coming clear, but she knew they were of a threatening nature. She just didn't know to whom or to what extent. Her biggest concern was the dreams started up about the same time as Sage's pregnancy. This worried her a great deal, yet she kept her fears to herself. She wasn't about to stir up any extra stress in Sage and Tommy's lives.

Tessy gathered up her notebook and put it off to the side. She needed to shake off this murky feeling. Sage was coming over for some lessons in an hour and she wanted this negative energy gone. After opening some windows, she went into the herbal kitchen and pulled down a smudge bundle of sage and lavender. She lit it, picked up her fanning feather and recited as she walked through the house:

"With this smudge I do plea
For protection of my home, pets and family
To keep evil and thievery far away
Anything unjust and wrong at bay
Only positive energy come with this smoke
Fill this space with truly loving and joyous folk
Any negativity and all things wrong
I banish you now. Be gone!
So mote it be."

By the time Sage arrived, the house was thoroughly cleansed and free of anything of ill will. Tessy decided, because of what was going on in the unknown, she would have Sage spend the day working on self-protection and cleansing. Tessy wanted Sage well versed and comfortable in these two areas for whatever was brewing. Sage never questioned Tessy on what lessons she deemed necessary.

"All right, love. It is very important to always keep yourself protected and cleansed with positive energy. Encircle yourself in as much white light as you can."

"So, how do I do that?"

"The best way to start is through meditation and yoga. I know you already have a wonderful routine and practice them daily, so if you keep that up your chakras will remain sharp and true."

"What do my chakras have to do with my protection?"

"First, you must keep your aura around ye clean and protected, that way your chakras stay aligned. This keeps you sharp and aware of your surroundings. Chakra work and aura work go hand in hand."

"Hmmm. I guess that makes sense. It's kinda what I do every day, but can you explain exactly what you mean?"

"Aye, the next time you are meditating, concentrate first on the energy around you. Visualize a bright protective white light surrounding you. Feel its vibration and warmth. Once you're comfortable, then start concentrating on your chakras. Make sure your root chakra feels completely grounded and safe. Visualize deep roots shooting straight down under you. Travelling up your body, your sacral chakra is next. It deals with your emotions, sexuality, reproduction, and creativity. Now, because of you being pregnant, this chakra might be a little off balance at the moment. So just concentrate on what emotions are bubbling up and try and face them head on."

"Ya, I might have a problem with that one. My emotions

seem to be all over the place right now." Sage chuckled.

"I know, love. There really isn't a whole lot we can do about that but do your best."

"Okay. I'll work on it."

"Aye. You'll be fine, love. Concentrating on the other chakras will definitely help. After the sacral is the solar plexus. It deals with intuition, will power, and gut instincts. You are very strong in all these areas so I would think your solar plexus is well aligned. That, however, does not mean you can skip over this chakra. When you hear someone say *trust your gut,* this is the chakra that will save you from harm."

"Yes, ma'am."

"Now comes the heart chakra. It connects with love, including self-love. Also, it represents your compassion and how you relate to people and things. Throat chakra is next. It deals with any type of communication, expression of self, truth, and creativity. Next your third-eye chakra awakens intuition and inner wisdom. It's your extrasensory perception. And, finally, we come to the crown chakra, which connects us to the Universe, the Divine, consciousness, and spirituality. Feel it pulling your head upwards and concentrate on your connection to the Divine."

"Thanks, Tess. The next time I meditate I will work on these."

"You're welcome, dear. 'Tis something we all should work a little harder on doing every day. And we need to keep ye and those wee babes as safe as we can."

"Is there something going on that I should know about, Tessy?"

Tessy was glad she had her back to Sage, at that moment. She wasn't sure she would have displayed her best poker face.

"No, love. Everything is just fine. 'Tis just part of your lessons."

17
The Perils of Pregnancy

Sage held her hair back as she leaned over the toilet for the fourth time that morning. Tommy stood at the bathroom door holding a glass of ice cubes, sympathetically watching. When she was finished, he handed her a towel, then the glass.

"Thanks." She slowly exhaled, then took the glass and sucked up an ice cube.

"I feel so helpless. I wish there was something I could do." Tommy groaned as he helped Sage into bed.

"I know, honey. It's okay. Dr. Kyle says the morning sickness shouldn't last much longer."

"Well, I sure hope not. It's been over thirteen weeks now." Tommy checked his watch. "Damn! I have to get to work. Are you going to be all right?"

"Yes. I'll be just fine. I'm feeling better already. Hopefully, that's it for a while."

"I hope so, babe. Make sure you try and eat something. I love you." Tommy kissed his wife on the forehead.

"I love you, too. Have a good day."

Sage lay propped up on the bed with puffy pillows supporting her. She listened as Tommy thundered down the stairs. The door slammed, the truck engine roared, faded, and then there was silence. Sage began to weep. She wondered how she was going to manage two babies all by herself when Tommy was at work.

Lately, she'd been feeling quite relaxed and happy but every once in a while, her hormones got the best of her. This morning was one of those times. She'd already cancelled a number of appointments this week due to morning sickness and was worried about finances on top of everything else. Sarah and Cherokee were really good at helping out at the shop when they could. But even though they were allowed responsible attendance at school, this was their senior year and it required their full attention. Sage did not want to be the cause of them missing any school.

She popped another ice cube in her mouth and eased herself out of bed. She stood in front of the mirror and stroked her growing belly. A faint smile emerged, and her mood brightened. At three months her bump was already quite prominent. Apparently, carrying twins did that.

Sage wriggled into her slippers and flip-flopped her way to the kitchen. She popped a piece of bread into the toaster and plugged in the kettle for some ginger tea. She felt better and really hoped that last trip to the bathroom was it for the rest of the day.

She finished her toast with a bit of pasteurized honey on it. It seemed like it was going to stay down. She poured her tea and took it over to the couch. She had photocopied a bunch of her Grandma Rose's documents and they were in a file on the coffee table. Sage set her cup down. She plumped up some pillows, got comfortable on the couch and picked up the file. It was mostly information on Haggerty names. She and Tommy had talked about names, but nothing too serious. Tommy didn't know much about his own family history and, therefore, had no set traditions. He was quite intrigued with Sage's colourful heritage and had no objections to following their interesting customs. His one and only request was, if they had a girl, could they somehow incorporate his mom's name, June. Sage lovingly agreed.

Sage found some unique names in her grandma's files. She couldn't believe that her grandma would think no one would be interested in this information. Sage found it fascinating; generation after generation naming their children after herbs. How could that not be interesting? And her mother had followed suit with Sage and her siblings, Rowan and Saffron. They were a continuation of this amazing tradition. Sage had no intention of breaking the chain.

By noon, Sage had regained her sea legs and was feeling pretty good. She had put in a couple of loads of laundry, had a shower and felt like she was ready to face the world. Her first appointment was at 1:10 p.m. She made herself a bowl of soup with crackers before she headed downstairs to the shop. It was snowing and she was grateful she didn't have to go out. She did, however, need a few groceries. She would try and remember to text Tommy after her appointment.

Her afternoon appointments were back-to-back. By 4:30 p.m., Sage was exhausted. Sarah and Cherokee stopped in after school just as Sage's last client was leaving.

"Oh, hello. Excuse us." Sarah and Cherokee stepped aside to

let the customer pass through the door.

"Hey guys," Sage greeted.

"Hey," the girls chimed.

"Whoa! Are you all right?" Cherokee blurted when she caught sight of Sage.

"Yes, thanks." Sage chuckled. "I'm just tired." She huffed as she plunked herself down on one of the reception chairs. "I think I'm done for the day," she continued. "I just have to clean up the treatment rooms and put the sheets and towels in the laundry."

"Well, Cherokee and I can take care of all that," Sarah said. "You go upstairs and lie down for a while."

"You girls don't have to do that."

"No, we don't. But we are. So go," Sarah teasingly ordered.

"Ahhh, thanks, you guys." Sage got up and headed toward the stairs, then stopped. "Oh, can you please take any calls that come in and lock up?"

"Of course. Go!" Sarah pointed to the stairs.

Sage laughed. "Okay, okay, I'm going. Thanks again."

Sage fell into a deep sleep and woke to darkness and the sound of Tommy coming in the door. "Damn!" She blurted. She saw the light flick on in the other room. "I'm sorry," she hollered out to Tommy.

Tommy rushed into the bedroom just as Sage was easing herself up. "Babe. Are you all right?" Tommy gathered her in his arms.

"Yes, honey. I am just fine," Sage assured.

"Have you been in bed all day?"

"Heavens no! Sarah and Cherokee came after school and closed up for me. I just laid down for a little rest and fell asleep. I'm sorry. I haven't made anything for supper. I meant to text you and get you to stop and pick something up."

"That's okay, babe. How do you feel about ordering pizza?"

"Actually, that sounds really good!"

"You must be feeling better." Tommy laughed.

18
Gifts of Neighbourly Goodwill

The days of November trickled into December. Everyone's life was busy with the hustle and bustle of the holiday season fast approaching. Well, for most everyone, but Sage.

Even though Sage's morning sickness had subsided, Dr. Kyle suggested she stay off her feet as much as possible. This meant she had to close down her treatment rooms. She was over at Tessy's for tea and bitterly complaining.

"How can I run a business and not have my treatment rooms open?" she wailed.

"Sage, dear. It will only be for a few months and 'tis for the good of ye and the wee babes. I'm sure all your clients understand."

"Yes, I know. Everyone has been so good about it, well, except Mrs. Chamberlain and she has never, ever, even booked an appointment. But, what if my clients find someone else in the meantime. I will lose them all."

"That's not about to happen, I'm sure."

"Well, it could."

"Sage, dear. There is no one within miles from here that even comes close to what you offer. I think you're pretty safe."

"Well, I just feel so bad that I'm letting everyone down."

"Love, you're not letting anyone down. You're taking care

of yourself. They survived without you for a good many years. They can survive for a few months. And yer available for any consultations and guidance to get them through."

"I suppose you're right. They all do know that. Thank you. That does make me feel a little better. Sarah and Cherokee offered to work a few days after school and on Saturdays. They will take messages and sell any product clients might need for themselves or for Christmas gifts."

Tessy gave Sage a big smile. "Say, I have a grand idea."

"What?" Sage gave her a funny look.

"Have ye thought about selling gift certificates?"

"Ooh, that's a great idea. People could purchase them for Christmas gifts."

"Aye. And, that way, they could use them after yer back. How 'bout we call the Ladyslipper Tribune, straight off, so they can place a little ad in time for this week's paper?"

"Oh Tessy, yes! Thank you. Can I use your phone?" By the time Sage left Ashling Manor she was feeling lighthearted and full of Christmas spirit.

Tessy spent the rest of the day making up her special Christmas baskets to deliver to friends and neighbours. This year she packed season potpourri, her famous gingerbread cookies, Yule Time tea, Heavenly Milk Bath Salts, and cookie cutter birdseed ornaments. On the weekend she'd had Emma and Becky over to help make the cookie cutter birdseed ornaments for their feathered friends.

Tomorrow, Tessy and Marshall were going over to their

neighbours, Danny and Betty Baker. They had a tree farm and Tessy and Marshall were ready to pick out their Christmas tree. Tessy wanted to make sure their basket was packed and ready to take over. The Baker's basket did include a little something extra for Danny, his absolute favourite, a Spicy Herbal Cheese Ball.

Another special basket Tessy always made up was for Mrs. Hobbs. This basket was an especially large one with extra food and gifts.

Marshall walked into the kitchen just as Tessy was putting the items in. He whistled. "Wow! Who's the lucky recipient of that one?"

Tessy laughed. "Well, 'tis for dear old Doris Hobbs. And I'm not sure I'd call her lucky."

"What do you mean?"

"Oh, she was married to a miserable old cuss. Folks say the kindest thing he ever did for Doris was die!"

Marshall chuckled. "Whoa! That's pretty harsh."

"Ye wouldn't say that if ye'd known old Walter. He was barely in the ground when the first thing Doris did was put indoor plumbing in the house. And that wouldn't be ten years ago, now."

"Seriously?"

"Aye. She lived in that old house all those years raising three boys with no running water. They weren't that poor. They had a pretty decent cattle farm. But he wouldn't spend a penny, well, 'cept on liquor. After he died, she tried for a couple of years to run the farm, but it just got too much for her. She sold the cattle and now rents out the land to her neighbour, Johnny Radford. Johnny clears her lane and keeps an eye on her. You know Johnny, I believe?"

"Yes, we golf together. Did none of the boys stay on?"

"Not a one! They all scattered to the wind as soon as they could. Can't say as I blame them much. They had it pretty rough with old Walter, but they left poor Doris alone with that rotten scoundrel."

"Well, if she sold the cattle and rents out the land she should be doing okay now, isn't she?"

"Aye. I think she makes out all right and has fixed up the house some. She's been wearing the same hat to church for twenty years. She's so accustomed to not having anything she has a difficult time spending any money on herself. Saving it for the boys I would imagine."

"Isn't Hobbs Hill where all the kids go tobogganing?"

"Aye 'tis. Walter used to chase them off something fierce when he was alive. Now, I think it's Doris's greatest pleasure to sit at her window all winter and watch them having fun. Bless her soul."

Marshall put his arm around Tessy and kissed her. "I love everything about you."

19
A Delightful Customer

With only a couple of Saturday's left before Christmas, Cherokee offered to work at The Healing Sage. She opened the door and flicked on the lights, then smiled. She loved how the first thing to hit her senses when she walked into Sage's clinic was the heavenly aroma of the essential oils. Cherokee took in a deep breath, then sighed.

She walked into the back, set down her schoolbooks and removed her coat. Even though she hoped it would be a busy day she also hoped to get some homework done. Sarah promised to come by a little later to help out and they planned to work on their assignments together.

Cherokee set straight to her morning duties. She plugged in the large fountain and checked the diffuser to see if it needed filling. It did. She took it apart, rinsed out the reservoir, filled it with some distilled water and went to Sage's cupboard of special mixed oils. There were so many wonderful ones to choose from. Since it was cold and flu season, Cherokee decided on a lovely blend called Sinus Cleanse. It was a combination of eucalyptus, rosemary, peppermint, lavender, and thyme. She counted out twelve drops into the distilled water, then put the diffuser back together and plugged it in. It produced a sweet and spicy, warm and comfortable, aroma.

Cherokee got her wish. Before she knew it, the shop was busy with people coming and going. Then the phone rang.

"Good morning, The Healing Sage," Cherokee cheerfully answered.

"Hi Cherokee. It's Sage. How are you doing?"

"Hey. Great. It's been really busy. Since you put that ad in the paper, gift certificates have been selling like crazy! I think I've sold seven already this morning."

"Wow. That's wonderful. Thank you for working for me, Cherokee. I really appreciate it."

"Oh, you're welcome. I think Sarah should be here pretty soon, too. And, if this keeps up it's a good thing." Cherokee chuckled.

"Well, you girls just remember to keep track of all your hours."

"You bet. Well, somebody just came in, better go."

"Okay. Bye and thanks again."

Cherokee was finishing up with her customer when Sarah walked in.

"Hey." Cherokee smiled.

"Hey." Sarah sniffed the air. "Man, it smells good in here."

"I know, right?"

"Have you been busy?" Sarah asked.

"Crazy busy."

"Wow. Great. Well, I'm here now so bring it on people." Sarah looked out the window. Cherokee laughed.

As Sarah went to the back to hang up her coat she called out, "I stopped in at Sheree's Café and picked up a couple of fresh bagels. I got our favourite, loaded herb with salmon cream cheese."

"Oh yum! Thanks. I'm starving. I'll be right there."

It was fairly quiet while the girls had their lunch. Sarah went out to the front a couple of times to help customers and let Cherokee have a break.

It slowed down shortly after one in the afternoon, so the girls pulled out their iPads and notebooks. Before they got too far along with their studies the bell on the door tinkled. They both looked up.

"I'll go," Sarah offered.

"No. It's okay. I'll go." Cherokee got up and went out.

The tiniest woman Cherokee had ever seen had her back to her. Then she recognized the hat.

"Well, hello, Mrs. Hobbs," Cherokee welcomed.

Mrs. Hobbs spun around. "Oh, hello, dear."

"How are you today?" Cherokee asked.

"Very well, thank you."

"How can we help you today?"

As soon as Sarah heard who it was, she came out to the front, as well. "Hello, Mrs. Hobbs." She always considered her the sweetest lady.

"Oh, you're here, too. Hello dear." Mrs. Hobbs offered her a warm smile. "You must forgive me. I'm sorry I can't remember your names. The perils of being old." She sighed.

Sarah smiled back at her. "That's okay. I'm Sarah Tucker and this is Cherokee Amiotte."

"Oh, yes, yes. Now I remember. Thank you, dear."

Cherokee asked again. "Is there something we can help you with today, Mrs. Hobbs?"

"Well now, I'm not sure. You see, I have a couple of gifts yet to buy and I'm plum stumped. I don't think I've ever been in this store." She glanced around. "What do you have here?"

Both Cherokee and Sarah smiled.

"Well, Mrs. Hobbs, who are you wanting to buy for?" Cherokee asked. "Like, what age, what gender?"

"Well now, let's see." Mrs. Hobbs dug into her purse, pulled out a list and held it up. "You have to keep lists when you get to my age." She tittered and looked down at the piece of paper. "There's my neighbour Johnny Radford and the lovely choir director, Mrs. Johnson. My, I do love how she makes that choir sing like angels. And, then there's my mail lady and that nice young man that makes grocery deliveries all the way out to my place. Can you imagine? He comes all that way and then he carries them straight into my kitchen. Of course, I give them all a box of my homemade preserves and baking, but we had a real good harvest this year, so I've got a little extra to spend. Now, I'm not rich by any means, so don't you girls be selling me the store."

The girls laughed.

"No, Mrs. Hobbs." Cherokee smiled. "We promise to keep the prices very reasonable. Let's see, I know Mr. Radford comes in for a massage occasionally. Maybe he'd like a gift certificate for one. We have the half-hour massage on special this month. He could use it after Sage gets back to work."

Sarah jumped in, "Oh, and Mrs. Johnson has a touch of eczema and uses one of Tessy's creams from time to time. Sage sells some here. You could get her a jar of that. And I'm pretty sure the delivery guy you are talking about is our friend, Jonathon. He's constantly bragging about how he has to shave everyday now." Sarah rolled her eyes and giggled.

"A shaving kit for him," Cherokee suggested. "It's a wonderful kit that includes all-natural soap, cream and aftershave. Trust me, he would love it."

"Oh my, those all sound like marvellous ideas. Thank you." Mrs. Hobbs sounded very pleased.

"Now, we only have the mail lady. Hmmm." Sarah walked over to one of the display cabinets and perused for a few minutes. "Oh, how about one or more of Tessy's herbal tea blends? There are some delicious ones here to choose from. We could do up a variety pack for her."

"Lovely, girls. Just lovely, I'll take everything that you have suggested. Thank you both so much for all your help."

The girls chatted with Mrs. Hobbs while they packaged up her order. They wished her a very Merry Christmas and watched her toddle down the street.

"Ahhh. I wish all our customers were like that. She's just the sweetest little lady ever," Sarah cooed.

"She sure is," Cherokee said, then added, "I hope I'm that

nice when I get old," Cherokee added.

"I hope so, too." Sarah laughed. "When we're in the seniors' home together I'm hoping to still want to be your best friend."

"Nice. Works both ways, you know." Cherokee playfully scowled. They shared a laugh and returned to their books.

20
Parcels and Preparations

Tessy was in the dining room wrapping Christmas gifts when she heard a tap at the front door. She went to the foyer and peeked out the curtains enough to see Tommy standing there with one large box in his arms and another one at his feet. She flung open the door.

"Well, Tommy dear! Come in. Come in. It's freezing out there. How are ye doing?"

"Fine. Thanks, Tessy."

"Oh my! What have ye got there? Do ye need some help?"

"No. No, I'm fine, thanks. Umm, I was wondering if I could hide a couple of gifts for Sage here?"

"Aye. Of course, ye can, my dear. Come. Bring them on into the dining room. That's where the pre-Christmas mess is, right at the moment." She chuckled. "So, what have ye got there, if you don't mind me asking?"

"Well, they're a couple of bassinets for the babies. Sage saw them online and fell in love with them. She said they were too expensive and quite impractical because the babies would grow out of them so fast. But right after she was looking at them, I caught her crying. I knew she really wanted them."

"Oh, Tommy dear. What a lovely gift. She will be so surprised."

"Well, I sure hope so. That's why I thought I'd better hide them over here."

"Aye dear, of course. Would like me to wrap them for ye?"

"Oh Tessy. That would be awesome if you don't mind? I'm not very good at wrapping. I will pay you for the wrapping paper."

"I don't mind one bit. And no, you'll not do anything of the kind. I've plenty of wrapping paper."

"Oh, thanks a lot. Well, I'd better get back to work." Tommy was already moving towards the foyer. "Thanks again." He smiled, stepped out the door and waved goodbye.

Tessy watched him head down the walk. "What a sweet lad he is. Sage is a very lucky young lass. It does my heart good." She returned to the dining room.

She had actually told a little white lie. She did need more paper before she wrapped the large parcels, but she wasn't about to have Tommy pay for it. They had enough expenses to worry about.

* * *

Tessy and Marshall carried down bins and boxes of ornaments from the attic for most of the morning. This was the day Danny Baker was dropping off the tree. It was always an exciting day when the tree arrived. It confirmed Christmas was truly here.

Ashling Manor had ten-foot-high ceilings, so Tessy always had one of the largest trees in Ladyslipper. This, of course, meant plenty of decorations. Marshall realized this was a bit of a drawback when he had to haul the bins down from the attic and then eventually, back up.

"Explain to me, again, why we have to have the biggest tree in town?" He complained as he set down a bin, then stood and stretched his back.

Tessy chuckled. "Well, love. It's not that we have to have the biggest tree in town. It's just nice to really appreciate it when it's all done and decorated. You'll see when it's finished. It will be lovely. Why don't ye take a break, love? Ye can start untangling the lights while I go up and get the last small bin."

"You call that taking a break?" Marshall grumbled.

Tessy giggled as she headed up the stairs. "I'll bring ye in a special eggnog when I get back."

"Does special mean what I hope it means?"

"Aye. I believe it does," she hollered back.

"Well, that will certainly help," he replied, then added under his breath, "But I don't think just one is going to do it."

Hours later, all the lights were on the tree as were most of the decorations. Christmas music played in the background as Tessy put the final touches here and there.

Marshall sat on the couch and enjoyed his third eggnog. He felt quite relaxed while he watched her. "You were right, sweetheart. It looks amazing. I don't know what I was grumbling about."

Tessy stood back and took a look at the magnificent display. "Aye. It does look grand, doesn't it? However, I think maybe 'tis more your eggnog talking right at the moment than ye." She laughed.

"Perhaps, but man, I'm really going to love sitting in here with you. We'll plug in the lights and get real cozy." Marshall had that devilish twinkle in his eye and boyish grin Tessy had never been able to resist. She stopped what she was doing and snuggled in close to her husband. At that moment, she didn't care whether it was Marshall or the eggnog talking.

* * *

Tessy's annual Christmas party was just days away. She had to admit, having someone help her with the preparations was a nice treat. Marshall took care of many of the details that Tessy was happy not to worry about. The walks were always shovelled, the blue bins were always emptied, and the water cooler was always filled. Yes, it was lovely to have a man around again. And, better yet, she rarely had to mention to him about any chores that needed to be done. She realized and appreciated how truly blessed she was.

* * *

The kids were on Christmas break and were over often to help or just hang out. The little girls spent their time with Tessy in the kitchen while Matt and his friends were over most days to help his grandpa with Brigid. It was wonderful to have the house filled with such energy. The Christmas spirit at Ashling Manor overflowed with a radiant glow of love and excitement.

Emma and Becky stood on stools at Tessy's kitchen island making up more cookie cutter birdseed ornaments to give as Christmas gifts. They also wanted to hang some in the trees at the downtown central park. They were quite concerned the birds didn't have enough to eat when it was cold. Tessy was greatly moved at how empathetic and kind the little girls were towards, not only their feathered friends, but all the animals.

"Grandma Tess?" Emma said with her head down intently stirring the mixture.

"Aye, love?"

"I just love these aprons that you made for me and Becky. Thank you."

"Ya, me too. Thank you." Becky piped.

"That's nice. You're very welcome, my dears. Glad you like them."

"Ya, they keep us from getting all dirty."

"Aye, they do. However, aprons do so much more than that. My granny, over in Ireland, was never without an apron."

"Why?" Emma stopped mixing and looked at Tessy.

"Well, an apron was much easier to wash than a dress and used less material to make. Money was tight, back then."

"Tight?" Emma interrupted.

"Scarce, not much money."

"Oh." Emma listened and went back to stirring.

"Aye. Granny used that apron to collect and carry all sorts of things. She brought eggs down from the chicken coop, kindling wood for the kitchen stove and carried all sorts of vegetables from the garden or apples from the orchard. When I fell down and hurt myself or just felt sad, she dried all my tears with her apron. I have such grand memories." Tessy laughed. "I remember a few times when she'd see some neighbours coming up the lane, she'd quickly dust the furniture with her apron and then quickly pull it off when the guests arrived. People nowadays would have a fit thinking of how many germs were on that apron. The only thing I ever caught from Granny's apron was love."

"Awhhh, what a nice story. I love your stories of the olden days." Emma smiled.

"Ya, me too," Becky agreed.

"Grandma Tess?" Emma asked.

"Aye, love."

"Can you and Grandpa take us down to the park when these are finished so we can hang them in the trees?"

"Aye love, we certainly can."

The two little girls smiled excitedly at one another and continued with their important task.

21
Another Unforgettable Party

Ashling Manor was a magickal sight. The candles were lit, the Christmas tree a twinkling wondrous vision, and the crackling fireplace warm and inviting.

Tessy wore an emerald-green velour jumpsuit. It was loose fitting and drawn at the waist with a satin sash. She tied a Christmas apron over her outfit to keep it unscathed. She was in the kitchen adding final touches to the platters of hors d'oeuvres when Marshall came up behind her. He wrapped his arms around her waist and buried his face into the nape of her neck. He exhaled a sexy growl. "Mmm, you smell as stunning as you look."

Tessy giggled and turned around. "Well, thank ye kind sir. You look rather dapper yourself." Marshall kissed her and continued to hold her.

Once again, the weather had not cooperated with Tessy's festivities. It was snowing hard and there was no sign of it letting up anytime soon.

"I fear there will be no horse-drawn sleigh rides for our Christmas guests this year." Tessy moaned.

"Well, there is one sleigh ride I shall never forget." Marshall was referring to the sleigh ride he and Tessy went on two years ago when he had popped the question.

Tessy smiled up at her adoring husband. "Aye. Nor shall I."

They were about to steal another kiss when the doorbell rang. They both went to the foyer to greet their first guests. It was Marshall's son, Dr. Kyle Tayse, and Becky's Mom, Susan.

"Merry Christmas!" everyone chimed in unison. They handed Tessy a beautiful poinsettia.

"Thank you. How lovely. I'll just go place it on the hutch in the dining room so everyone can enjoy it." Tessy took the plant while Marshall helped Susan off with her coat. They were making their way into the living room when the doorbell rang again. It was Marshall's daughter, Penny with Jim, and right behind them was Sage and Tommy. Soon Ashling Manor was filled with season's greetings and Christmas cheer. The snow building up outside didn't seem to deter any of the guests or dampen their holiday spirit. Danny and Betty Baker came and apologized for not showing up with their team of horses.

"Don't ye fret another minute. 'Tis a nasty night out there. Not fit for human nor beast. We're glad to have ye come join the indoor fun this year, Danny boy."

Betty soon took her favourite spot at the piano and the singing began. As the storm roared on, guests merrily mingled, while others stood around the piano carolling. Tessy and Sage stood off to the side and watched the festivities.

"Oh, I see Mrs. Hobbs came this year." Sage smiled.

"Aye. The Radford's brought her. She's such a dear soul. I'm so glad to see her finally getting out and mixing a mite."

"Ya, she's a sweetheart. It's sure good to see Susan so happy, too. Dr. Kyle is such a nice guy and he's great with Becky. Do you think he'll pop the question soon?"

"I'd be thinkin' it shan't be long now." Tessy smiled and winked.

"Well, everyone seems to be having a really good time. However, if one more person pats my belly, I'm going to lose it." Sage playfully scorned.

Tessy chuckled. "They're just so happy for ye, dear. We all are." Tessy teasingly patted Sage's tummy and moved on to her other guests.

About an hour and half into the party, the front door burst open, and a breathless Sarah barged in. Marshall ran to her. "Sarah! What's the matter? Take your time. Catch your breath."

Most everyone from the living room stopped and stared at the girl bent over gulping for air. "The kids," Sarah gasped. "Emma and Becky are missing," she exclaimed, still trying to catch her breath.

"Missing? What do you mean missing?" Marshall's tone bordered on frantic.

By now, Tessy, along with Jim and Penny, Kyle and Susan, had reached the foyer.

Tessy placed her hand on Sarah's back to calm her. "Sarah, dear. What's gone on? What happened to the children?"

"I don't know!" Sarah cried. "They said they were going out into the backyard to play in the snow. It wasn't storming too badly when they went out. Then it got worse, so I went to call them in and they weren't there! Matt, Brendon, and Cherokee are all out looking for them. I came to get Mom and Dad." Sarah looked at her parents and broke into tears. "I'm so sorry. I never would have let them go outside if I'd known they would go off somewhere."

Jim was already putting on his coat and helping Penny with hers. Penny could see how upset her daughter was. She put her arm around Sarah. "I know, sweetheart. We'll find them."

Soon there were a number of people getting dressed to help. Tommy was already in his truck making tracks down the lane for people to get out.

"I'll go get some flashlights." Marshall ran to the kitchen.

"Leave one for me." Tessy hollered as she ran upstairs to change into something warm. Tessy returned back downstairs to the few remaining guests. Sage and the older guests were truly concerned.

"What can we do to help?" Mrs. Hobbs asked as she pulled Tessy aside.

"Doris dear, it would be a grand if ye could remain here in case the children happen to arrive or phone. And, if you could please keep an eye on Sage that would be wonderful. We want to make sure she and those babies stay safe."

"Yes, of course. I'd be glad to do that," she answered.

"Thank ye kindly. Hopefully we'll hear something soon." Tessy patted Mrs. Hobbs on the arm.

Tessy went to the kitchen to get the flashlight Marshall had left her. She spotted the two little aprons Emma and Becky had been wearing the other day. She grabbed them, then went out to the porch where the dogs had been quarantined during the party. She hurried into her coveralls, heavy coat, and boots. The dogs sensed the excitement and were bouncing by the time Tessy was dressed. She calmed them as much as possible and put the aprons under their noses.

"That's right, get a good sniff. Now, go find the girls. Where are the girls?" She repeated over and over as she opened the door and let them fly. The dogs tore across the backyard and into the grove of trees. Tessy grabbed a quilt from the porch and the sleigh just outside the door. She followed as fast as she could, but with the deep snow she wasn't making much headway. She could hear the dogs, but they were out of sight. With the storm raging it was difficult to detect exactly where they were. She stopped to listen. One minute they sounded as if they were to the north, then to the south. She heard a loud "caw" right above her and looked up. It was Henry!

"Great leaping leprechauns! Henry! What in the devil are ye doing out in this?"

He cawed again and flew a few trees away where Tessy could still see him. She followed. All along the way, Henry flew off but stayed within sight. The dogs' barks became louder. Tessy shone her flashlight in the direction of the frantic barking. She was sure she could make out their figures in the dark. They were over by the old wooden grain bin, long forgotten and hidden in the overgrown bushes. As she approached, she heard faint cries for help. She ran to the bin.

"Emma, Becky! Is that ye?"

"Yes! Yes!" they both cried.

"Don't cry, my dears. I'll get ye out."

The door to the bin was closed and blocked with fresh driven snow. Tessy pried an old wide board leaning up against the bin out of the snow and started digging. The dogs were furiously digging alongside her. Before too long, with Tessy pulling the door while the girls pushed from inside, they were able to get it open enough for the girls to squeeze out. There were plenty of tears and just as many hugs. Tessy got the girls calmed down and seated on the sleigh with the quilt tucked around them. It wasn't easy pulling them, but Tessy took it slow. She looked up and thought she saw flashes of light. She called out and waved her flashlight. The light got brighter. It was Marshall and Jim.

Tessy was so relieved. "How did ye find me?"

"Doris watched you head out this way with the dogs, so I was pretty sure what you were up to." Marshall smiled.

"Oh, thank the good Lord." Tessy fell into his arms. Jim was hugging the girls.

"Well, let's get these wee rascals back to Ashling Manor to warm up." Tessy sighed.

She looked up to see if Henry was anywhere nearby. He was gone, probably safely tucked back into his cozy nest deep within the large fir tree behind Ashling Manor. Tessy would remember to leave him an extra special treat tomorrow.

Emma and Becky were soon snuggled in blankets in front of the fireplace with a cup of hot chocolate. Marshall and Kyle checked them for hypothermia. They both concluded the girls were fine but agreed they were found just in the nick of time.

Once word spread that the little girls were found safe and sound, Tessy's guests said their goodnights and went home. The only ones left were the girls' parents. Emma and Becky knew they were in big trouble.

Emma looked up from her hot chocolate. "I'm sorry," she offered teary eyed.

"I should say," her mother scolded. "What were you two thinking? You could have frozen to death out there!"

"Well, Becky and I wanted to sneak over and see what the grown-up party was like. So, we told Sarah we wanted to play outside for a while. We started to walk over here the back way through the bushes. But then it got really stormy, and we couldn't see. We got lost."

"I'm sure that was very scary. But, young lady, you are so lucky your big sister cared enough to check on you when it got miserable out. You had half the town out looking for you."

"Yes ma'am. Sorry."

Penny continued, "You owe Sarah a big apology when you get home. You lied and scared her half to death!"

"I know. I will. I promise." Emma nodded.

Susan looked at her daughter. "Becky, you also owe everyone an apology. Especially Sarah when you see her again. And, if you still think you are sleeping over at Emma's tonight, you are sadly mistaken."

"Yes ma'am." Becky sheepishly looked over at her friend and shrugged. She then looked around the room. "Sorry everyone."

The parents gathered up the girls and took them home, which left Tessy and Marshall alone. Tessy went out to the kitchen to tidy up when she noticed everything had pretty much been done. "Oh, Sage and that sweet Mrs. Hobbs."

She opened the fridge door and pulled out a couple of juicy pieces of ham. She looked over at Duke and Darby sound asleep on their beds, contently snoring, quite oblivious to their earlier heroic deed. She smiled and put the ham back. A special breakfast would certainly be in order.

Marshall came out to the kitchen and wrapped his arms around Tessy and sighed. "Well, you've done it again."

Tessy looked puzzled. "Done what again, love?"

"Hosted another unforgettable party at Ashling Manor!" They laughed and walked arm in arm out of the kitchen.

* * *

By the following dawn the storm had ended. The bright morning sun caused the fresh blanket of snow to glisten like a million diamonds. Marshall was out shovelling the walks when he looked up to see Tessy bundled up and heading out with a basket.

"Where are you off to, darling?"

"I'm off to find Henry to give him his Christmas treats. Shan't be long, love."

Marshall, not quite getting the relationship between Tessy and *that bird*, just shook his head and continued on with his task.

Tessy ploughed through the deep snow across the backyard

and into the grove. She'd locked the dogs in the back porch with their special breakfast of scrambled eggs and ham. She wanted to share some alone time with Henry. She made her way to his fir tree and stood below looking up towards his nest.

"Henry," she quietly called, then waited.

Henry poked his head out and looked down at his trusted friend. He hopped out onto the branch, heavily laden with snow. His movement and body weight caused the branch to bounce, and a big plop of snow fell to the ground, barely missing Tessy. She stepped back.

"Well, good mornin' to ye," she greeted. "I've a few treats here for ye. I don't imagine ye know what a grand help ye were to us last night, nor do ye probably care. I just want to thank ye and leave these few things for ye. Ye are a grand friend and we're blessed to have ye here with us at Ashling Manor."

She reached into her basket and began to scatter the treats on the ground under the tree. There were pumpkin seeds, peanuts in the shell, grapes, cranberries, cut up apple, a few chunks of raw stewing beef and, of course his favourite, hardboiled eggs. When she emptied the basket, she looked up and smiled.

"Well, Merry Christmas, Henry dear. These treats should last ye a day or two. I'll be back to visit soon." Tessy turned and headed towards the house.

She had only taken a few steps when she heard a rustling. She looked back to see Henry on the ground checking out his windfall. He looked up and gave a loud "caw" before he returned to sorting through which of the gifts he would savour for breakfast.

Tessy's heart was full.

22
Meddling, Mucus and Magus

A blessed Christmas came and went at Ashling Manor. Tessy and Marshall hosted Christmas Day complete with turkey and all the trimmings. The dining room table was as picturesque as any Currier and Ives. Marshall sat at one end of the long table with Tessy at the other. Seated between was Jim, Penny, Sarah, and Matt, Kyle with Susan, and of course, Sage and Tommy. The two wee girls begged to sit at their very own little table, decorated and set off to the side.

Tessy had planned on inviting Mrs. Hobbs but, miraculously, this year her boys and their families all came home to be with her. Unbeknownst to most, after Marshall fell privy to Doris's life history, he had a chat with her doctor. That just happened to be Dr. Kyle Tayse. Kyle made a phone call to the son Doris had listed as her contact. He expressed his concerns regarding her mental well-being, especially during the holiday season.

"Blessed be!" was all Tessy could say. With a little meddling from her husband, it was the most beautiful Christmas Mrs. Hobbs had ever experienced. Doris even found an anonymous gift under her tree. She opened it to find a lovely new hat.

Her magickal Christmas didn't end there. The annual Boxing Day toboggan party on Hobbs Hill was another joyous affair. This was the first time Doris's grandchildren had ever been out to the farm. The Ladyslipper children welcomed them whole-heartedly, bringing extra toboggans and loads of blissful laughter. Even Mrs. Hobbs bundled up and enjoyed the day outside at the hill. Her sons hauled an old picnic table out for people to sit. They then lit a huge bonfire to keep everyone warm. Yes, Hobbs Hill would be a more pleasurable place for winter fun from this day forward. It was another new beginning in Ladyslipper.

The days passed in a holiday haze and soon it was New Year's Eve. Tessy and Marshall opted to stay home and quietly ring in the New Year. Marshall wasn't feeling very sociable. He was battling a nasty head cold that seemed to be travelling down into his chest.

"Achoo! Ugh." Marshall moaned and blew his nose.

"Poor dear." Tessy handed him a fresh tissue. "Are ye sure ye wouldn't just rather pop off to bed, love?"

"And miss New Year's Eve with my best girl! Not in your life." Marshall used as much enthusiasm and humour as he could muster.

Tessy chuckled. "Well, at least let me go fix ye a nice cup of hot water with lemon, ginger, and honey."

"Ooh, do you know what would be even better? How about a nice hot rum toddy?" Marshall croaked out before he coughed.

Tessy chuckled again, shaking her head. "Aye. That probably wouldn't harm ye none."

Tessy went to the kitchen to make a couple of toddies. As she was mixing the ingredients she fell deep in thought.

What shall this New Year bring about? Two Blessed wee babes, to be sure. But what else is brewing? She was thinking about the murky, foul presence that seemed to be getting more prominent with every passing day. Her dreams were getting darker and heavier each night.

She placed the rum toddies and a plate of gingerbread cookies on a tray and carried them in to where her husband was lounging. The fireplace blazed yet Marshall still had a throw draped over him. He really wasn't feeling well. Tessy didn't want Marshall trying to talk so she suggested they watch a movie. They decided on a romantic comedy as it was more than likely Marshall would doze off anyway.

The movie ended and Tessy looked over at her snoring husband. She gathered up the dirty dishes and carried the tray into the kitchen. The dogs wanted out. She flicked on the backlight and watched them bound out into the deep snow. She stood watching for a few minutes when she heard something behind her. She turned expecting to see Marshall but instead a flash of purple passed through the length of the kitchen. She closed her eyes and shook her head, then looked again. The bright light was gone, but a glowing aura remained. She walked through it with her palms open as if brushing the coat of the softest rabbit. The warmth filled her soul, and she knew it was a shield of positive energy. There was another noise. Tessy spun around. Marshall stood in the doorway.

"I guess I must have dozed off," he said in a nasally moan followed by a cough. "What's the matter?"

"Nothing, love. Let's go to bed. I'll let the dogs in."

"But it's not quite midnight yet," he whined.

"I think you'll enjoy the New Year a mite better in the mornin' after you've had a good sleep."

Marshall turned and went upstairs without any more of an argument. Tessy remained in the kitchen a while longer. She didn't really know what she was expecting to happen, but she was hoping for something. A sign, a feeling, a vision, just something. Anything.

She let the dogs in. They went straight to their beds without being told and stared across the room both caulking their heads. Tessy looked in that direction, nothing. She waited another twenty minutes while she tidied up the kitchen. The clock struck midnight. The New Year had just begun. Tessy turned out the lights and took one more long look. The faint purple hue of the aura remained through the darkness. She knowingly smiled.

23
A Big Decision

"The babies are doing very well, Sage," Dr. Kyle assured. "The ultrasound will tell us more." He swung his stool away from her as he discarded his gloves into the trashcan. Sage slowly lowered her legs from the cold stirrups and pushed her gown down as far as it would go. She tried to sit up.

"Whoa! Wait right there, missy. I'm not done with you yet." Dr. Kyle was at the sink washing his hands. He pulled a couple of sheets out of the towel dispenser and looked over at his patient.

"Now, let's take a good look at you."

She eased herself back onto the table. He strapped the blood pressure cuff around Sage's upper arm and placed the stethoscope in his ears to listen to her pulse. He looked up at the monitor. "Blood pressure is a little off, but not bad. We'll just keep an eye on it. Let's see. You're halfway through your second trimester so that means you're halfway there. I see you're suffering with some hemorrhoids. Do you need me to prescribe something for that?"

"No. I've got some cream at home. Thanks." Sage groaned.

Dr. Kyle smiled. "Any other complaints?"

"Oh, where do I begin?" Sage groaned again and rubbed her belly. "I'm having terrible heartburn lately. A couple of weeks ago I had lots of energy and now I don't seem to have any. My feet are swollen most days and my back is killing me. I can't seem to get comfortable in bed so I'm not sleeping that great, either." She didn't bother mentioning the nightmares she'd been having. *Not much he could do about that*, she thought.

"Most everything sounds pretty normal except for your lack of energy. During this period, you should have a lot more. I would like to run a couple of tests. I think your iron might be down making you a little anaemic. For your heartburn, try and stay away from any spicy food or anything with a lot of sugar. Antacids should also help. Have you tried a large body pillow to help you get comfortable in bed?"

"No."

"Well, I'd suggest you pick one up. I think that would help immensely. For the swelling in your feet, less salt, drink lots of water and put your feet up above your heart. Also, wearing good quality, comfortable shoes, even when you're in the house."

"I can barely fit into my slippers these days, so finding shoes might be a bit of a challenge."

"Well, see what you can find. I think the extra support would do you some good. Now, if there's nothing else, let's go get you ready for your ultrasound. Are you wanting to know the sex of the babies?"

"Yes! Tommy and I want to know but we're going to keep it a secret."

"Well, we should be able to tell for sure today."

"Really?" Sage let out a little squeal.

Dr. Kyle laughed and nodded. "Okay then. Let's go. Is Tommy in the waiting room?" He helped Sage down from the examining table.

"Yes. Would you please go get him?" Sage asked as she grabbed the back of her gown holding it tightly closed, then shuffled out of the examining room.

The ultrasound was a success. The babies looked healthy, well situated and of about equal size. The sex of each was also determined. Tommy and Sage were thrilled. By the time they got home Sage was exhausted but ecstatic. She took the ultrasound pictures out of the envelope to look at one more time. "Look Tommy. Just look. Aren't they beautiful?"

Tommy was more than happy to sit with Sage and beam at his soon-to-be little family. He was able to convince Sage to lean back on the couch while he went and got a pillow for under her legs. "Can I get you anything, babe?" he asked.

"Maybe a glass of water, please. I'm supposed to be drinking lots of water."

In the days that followed, even with Sage drinking extra water and watching her salt intake, her legs and feet were quite swollen. She had awful nightmares and had started to experience minor contractions.

Tommy was worried, especially when he had to go to work. He called to see if Tessy could come over and check on Sage during the day. Tessy was more than happy to pop over and spend a few hours a day with her.

"Now, dear. Can I make ye a nice cup of hot water and lemon?" Tessy asked as she gently tucked another pillow under Sage's legs.

"That sounds great. Sure, if you don't mind."

"Mind?" Tessy scoffed. "'Course I don't mind."

"Ooh no!" Sage cried.

"What, dear? What's the matter?" Tessy rushed to Sage's side.

"Oh, I just had another one of those contractions. I'm so worried. It's way too early."

"Are they painful at all?" Tessy asked.

"No. Not so much painful. Just kinda strange."

"Well dear, if they're not painful it sounds like you're having what's called, Braxton Hicks contractions. They are quite normal for this stage and actually a really good thing. They are like warmup exercises for your uterus."

"Oh. I remember reading about them in those books you gave us. So that's what you think this is?"

"Aye, dear. I'm pretty sure. You should be just fine."

"Now, if I could just find some shoes for my swollen feet. Man, they are so sore. Dr. Kyle suggested I try and find some comfy shoes to wear. He said I should even be wearing them in the house. But, where on earth would I find shoes to fit these monsters!" Sage lifted her foot to show Tessy.

"Oh goodness. Poor dear. Well, ye know, Penny has some wonderful shoes in The Lady's Slipper. I should just give her a call right now and see if she has anything in the store that might work for ye. What size are you normally?"

"That would be great. Thanks. I'm a size seven."

Sage listened to Tessy's side of the conversation. It didn't sound promising. When Tessy hung up, she looked over at Sage.

"Well, love. Unfortunately, Penny doesn't have anything like that, right at the moment. But she's placing a big order a little later today and said she will bring in a couple of options for you to choose from. She gave me the website for you to take a look and see what you think."

"That's awesome. Thank you."

"I'll pop down in a few days and see if they're in."

"I don't know what I'd do without you, Tess. Now, if you could just figure out a way to help me with these nightmares, life would be good." Sage groaned.

Tessy had gone back into the kitchen to get Sage's lemon water. She looked up from pouring the hot water. "Nightmares? What nightmares?"

"I've been having terrible dreams for weeks now."

Tessy set the cup down on the coffee table in front of Sage. "Tell me about them. Don't leave anything out."

Sage told Tessy about all the dark and scary dreams in great detail. Much to Tessy's dismay, they were incredibly similar to the ones she had. She said nothing to Sage and told her it was probably hormones.

Tessy continued to drop over daily to check on Sage. She did not seem to be getting any better and Tessy insisted on Sage making another doctor's appointment. On the day it was scheduled, Tessy took her so Tommy didn't have to miss work. Dr. Kyle examined her and concluded she should stay off her feet. He was worried about her climbing up and down so many stairs.

"I live in an apartment on the second floor. How can I not climb stairs?" Sage complained to Tessy in the car on the way home.

Tessy remained silent but her mind was reeling. She got Sage back up to their apartment and stayed until Tommy got home.

When Tessy got back to Ashling Manor she went straight out to the shop to find Marshall. He was leaning into Brigid's engine.

"I'm home, love." Tessy hollered over the music Marshall had blaring.

Marshall leapt up and banged his head on the hood. He cursed and grabbed the back of his head.

Tessy silently giggled. "Oh, love. Sorry. Are ye all right?"

"Yes," he grumbled, still rubbing his head. He went over and turned down the radio.

"I've something I need to talk to ye about, love."

"Oh. Okay. Can it wait a few minutes? I'm almost done here. Then I can get cleaned up and come in. We can sit and have a drink before supper."

"Aye. That sounds perfect. See ye in a bit, then." Tessy turned and walked out.

Tessy was so happy when the new shower was, finally, installed in the Quonset bathroom. It certainly made for less mess and easier cleaning in their master bathroom.

It took a little longer than Tessy expected but as promised, Marshall appeared fresh and clean, ready to talk. Marshall poured Tessy a glass of wine and twisted the top off a beer for himself before he sat down at the kitchen table.

He handed Tessy her wine. "Okay. I'm all ears. What's up?"

Tessy smiled. "Thank you. Well, I guess I'll just get right to it. I think Sage and Tommy should come live here, with us, at Ashling Manor. At least until the babies come and possibly for a while after."

Marshall was in the middle of taking a gulp of beer and choked out, "Whoa! What?"

"Aye. I know it will be a little bit of an inconvenience in our daily life, but Sage should not be on her own and Kyle said he doesn't want her going up and down any stairs." Tessy stated, trying to defend her case.

"Well darling, if you haven't noticed we have stairs. Where are they going to sleep?"

"I've been thinking about that. What I thought we could do is move a bed down here in the den for Sage. Tommy could sleep in one of the guest rooms upstairs."

"The den!" Marshall exclaimed.

"I know. I know. But we could still use the library. There is a pocket door between the den and the library that we could close for privacy. Both for us and for her."

Marshall was quiet for a few minutes. "Well, I guess we could think about it."

"Thank ye, love. I haven't mentioned anything to them yet, so I'll let you think it over for a couple of days before I do."

"Okay. Just give me a few days to wrap my head around this. It's been a while since I've had crying babies in the house."

Marshall looked a little green around the gills.

Tessy chuckled. She got up and hugged her husband around the back of his neck and kissed his cheek.

24
If the Shoe Fits

Penny Tucker unlocked the door to her shoe store, The Lady's Slipper. She flicked on the lights and glanced around. Even though she'd had the shop for a year now, it was still a thrill to step into it every morning. It brought her great joy and a sense of pride. She was happy knowing it gave her little community a place to buy good quality shoes. Especially, when their only other option was to drive over an hour into the city.

She put on a pot of coffee and got straight to work dusting and tidying up. She needed to clear some space as she had a big order arriving. She was quite excited to see the newest spring line. Penny had recruited Sarah and Cherokee to help pick out the latest fashions for the younger crowd and Tessy helped with some suggestions for the more mature.

Other than a couple of neighbours stopping in to say hi, it was a pretty quiet morning. She was in the back going over some invoices when she heard the bells above the door tinkle. She looked out the office window to see who it was.

"Oh great," Penny groaned under her breath. She got up and went out to the front.

"Good morning, Mrs. Chamberlain. How are you today?"

Mrs. Chamberlain glanced up at Penny. "Well enough, I suppose." She sneered, while stomping the snow off her boots.

"What can I help you with this morning?" Penny smiled.

Mrs. Chamberlain looked around the store then snorted. "Well, by the looks of things, not much."

"Oh, sorry," Penny apologized then, continued, "I know the shelves look a little sparse right at the moment. I'm expecting a large shipment today. It should be here any moment now."

"Not a minute too soon, I'd say," Mrs. Chamberlain curtly replied. She casually picked up and inspected shoes along one wall, then put them back as she went. She eventually found a style she appeared to be interested in. She checked the price. "I'd like to try these on in an eight and a half."

"I don't believe I have any of those left in an eight and a half." Penny winced.

"Of course, you don't." Mrs. Chamberlain huffed. "Why would I expect any different?"

"Well, just in case, I'll go check in the back. Excuse me." Penny came back out a few minutes later. "I'm sorry, I don't. But I do have something very similar in an eight and a half. Would you like to see them?"

"No! I don't want something similar. I want these. If you order them in, when can I expect them?"

"Oh, Mrs. Chamberlain, those were from our fall collection, and I believe they have been discontinued. That's why they are on for such a great price."

"I don't know why I even try to shop in this town!"

"Well, we really do appreciate you buying local—" Penny began. A loud banging at the back door interrupted her. "Oh,

139

excuse me. That will be my order. I'll be right back." And she started to head off.

"Wait," Mrs. Chamberlain barked. "I'll take a look at those similar ones you were talking about."

"Certainly, Mrs. Chamberlain. But if you can wait just a minute while I get my order. I'll be right back with those shoes."

"Humph! Some service."

Penny rolled her eyes as she opened the back door. She signed for her order and held the door open for the delivery person. It took a few minutes, but she got back to her disagreeable customer before she left.

"Here we are, Mrs. Chamberlain. I hope you find these to your liking. If you'll have a seat, I'll help you try them on."

Mrs. Chamberlain sat down while Penny assisted her. Mrs. Chamberlain got up, looked in the mirror and walked around in them for a few minutes.

"I suppose they'll have to do. I'm certainly not going to find anything else. Unless there's something in one of those boxes." She brightened.

"I'm sorry, Mrs. Chamberlain. I have to process the order before I can sell anything. They should all be out on the shelves in a day or two."

"Of course. Again, why would I expect anything different? Fine. I'll take these. But I want them at the same price as the ones I originally wanted but couldn't get."

Penny, knowing there'd be no point in arguing, just sighed. "All right, Mrs. Chamberlain. I guess I could do that."

"I should think." Mrs. Chamberlain glared.

They were just finishing up at the counter when Tessy walked in.

Mrs. Chamberlain turned. "Humph. Looks like anyone can walk in here."

Tessy smiled. "Well, hello Margaret. How are you today?"

Mrs. Chamberlain gave another, "Humph," picked up her parcel and added, "I didn't see any witch's boots so maybe you're wasting your time."

Tessy never missed a beat. "Well, of course not. Penny, keeps all the magick slippers in a special room at the back."

The shocked Mrs. Chamberlain stared at Tessy for a moment not sure what to believe, then with one final huff, she walked out.

Penny waited for her to close the door before she let out a hearty laugh.

Tessy smiled. "I know I shouldn't egg her on like that but sometimes I just can't help myself."

Penny laughed again. "Well, I love it. And she certainly deserves any ribbing she gets. How are you?" The two women hugged.

"Grand thank ye, love. Isn't it thrilling news about Kyle and Susan getting engaged?"

"Yes! Finally! I didn't think my brother was ever going to get around to officially popping the question." Penny laughed.

"Aye. I guess he decided New Year's Eve was the perfect time. How special."

"Looks like they are talking about a fall wedding."

"Aye, I cannot imagine a better time. What a blessed year this is turning out to be. We have babies to arrive in the spring and a wedding in the fall. More new beginnings for our wee town. Oh, speaking of babies," she continued, "I just popped in to see if you've received those comfy stretchable shoes for Sage's poor swollen feet, yet?"

"Oh, yes. They should be in the order I just received a few minutes ago. I haven't had time to open any of the boxes. The order came in when I was helping Mrs. Chamberlain. If you're able to wait I can open a couple of boxes and see if I can find them."

"Oh, love. Thank ye, but I'm sure you have to check everything first, don't ye?"

"Well, yes, normally. But for you I can certainly make an exception. And, besides, they're already paid for."

"If you're sure, love. That would be grand. Thank ye. Do ye need some help?"

"Sure, that would be great. Let's get these boxes opened." Penny beamed. She handed Tessy a utility knife and they both got down to business. Penny was more than happy to have someone there with her to ooh and ahh over the new shoes.

They eventually found Sage's order. Tessy removed them out of the box to examine them. She gently pulled and stretched them to make sure they had enough give.

"I think these will be dandy. Just what Sage needs on those poor feet."

"Great. I sure hope they do the trick." Penny smiled.

"Well, dear. Looks like I've made as big a mess as I can. So, I must be off." Tessy chuckled.

"Not at all. Thank you so much for your help. You have saved me from staying late tonight."

The two women hugged.

Penny watched Tessy carry on down the street. *What would the world be like without Tessy McGuigan?* she thought. *Not one I'd like to be in, that's for sure.* Penny shook her head and went back to her task at hand.

25
Nilrem

In the snowy weeks that followed Tessy's enlightening experience on New Year's Eve, she noticed faint purple orbs and auras throughout her house. After past months of nightmares and uneasy feelings she found them comforting. She did, however, continue to stay present and aware.

Marshall buckled on the decision to have the kids move in with them. Tessy knew he was actually looking forward to it but never bothered to bring that up. She let him continue on with his grumpy façade to save face.

It had been a couple of months since Marshall had been to Winnipeg and there was some important paperwork that needed his attention, or so he said. She knew the paperwork could have been done electronically. Tessy was pretty sure Marshall was just feeling a little homesick for Winnipeg and missing a good visit with Dotty and Bert. She would have gladly gone with him this trip but with Sage's delicate condition she felt she was needed here. He stood in the foyer with his bags in hand.

"Well darling, I'd better get going. I don't want to miss my flight. Sorry, I have to go, again. I shouldn't be any longer than a few days. I just want to get this legal stuff all cleared up and out of the way."

"Aye, love. I agree. I'd love to go with ye but with Sage and

Tommy moving in soon I just don't think it's the right time."

"I know, darling. So, will I be coming home to a house full?" he asked.

"Well, there's no set date, yet, but there is a possibility." Tessy winced.

Marshall laughed. "Okay. Well, keep me posted. I hope everything goes well."

"Don't ye worry about us here, we'll be fine as frog's fur."

Marshall set his bags down and pulled Tessy into his arms. "I love you." He kissed her long and tenderly.

Tessy stood at the open door and watched him drive out the lane. She felt a nudge at her hand. She glanced down to see Duke looking up at her.

"Oh, ye wee darlin'. Come. Let's get ye a nice treat."

Tessy busied herself with cleaning and getting things ready for Sage and Tommy. She finished dusting in the library and moved into the den when she felt a presence. It wasn't her beloved deceased husband, Dermot, because there was no scent of Old Spice. The room filled with a brilliant purple light. It flashed, snapped and popped with glowing energy. As it dissipated Tessy saw a shape take form. It was the odd little wizard that followed Tessy throughout Ireland on her honeymoon. He appeared as he did when they'd first met. He was garbed in his hooded cloak of shimmering dark green and purple with pagan etched gold trim.

Tessy let out a soft gasp and then a chuckle. "So 'tis ye that has been gadding 'bout my house!"

The wizard returned the chuckle. "Aye, but 'tis for good

reason. We've much to discuss."

"Come. Sit." Tessy pointed to a couple of easy chairs in the den.

It took a minute for the little wizard to climb into the chair and get comfortable. Then he started. "I'd be thinkin' the first thing you'd be wantin' to know is me name. Well, they call me Nilrem of the Cauldron of Hues. I've followed ye 'bout since ye were just a wee sprig. Since the very beginnings of your schooling in spells and enchantments. I remained mostly in Ireland after ye left but kept an eye on your progress here, as well. I knew you'd one day be needin' me services in the homeland. But now, now, you're needin' me services right here."

"What do ye mean, Nilrem? What has happened?"

"'Tis not what has happened but what is about to happen."

"Nilrem! Stop talking in riddles and please tell me what is brewing. I've been having many a bad dream but can't make head nor tail out of them."

"'Tis Agnes. She never crossed over. She swears to take those wee Haggerty twins who are 'bout to bless this world."

"No!" Tessy exploded. "Not while I have one more breath in my body will that wretched hag touch those wee babes. Agnes has taken enough from my life. She will not take another soul."

Agnes was a distant relative of Tessy's. She lived in Ireland and was responsible for the death of Tessy and Kennan's parents over forty years ago.

While Tessy was on her honeymoon, she and Keenan tracked down Agnes to question her. She was mentally unstable and very feeble at the time. She died shortly after her confession.

Nilrem smiled. He was relieved to see Tessy so fired up. "That's why I've come. I'm confident that between the pair of us we can stop her in her tracks. You're more powerful than you know, Tessy McGuigan. The sparks and aura that radiated from your sudden blow up just now was enough to confirm what I already know to be true."

Tessy got up and paced the room. Her mind spun. "Protection. Protection. What do I need for protection?" she muttered.

"The first thing ye need is to get a grip on yourself, woman." Nilrem barked.

"Aye. Of course." Tessy sighed. She took in a few deep breaths and calmed.

Nilrem gave Tessy a minute then said, "All right. Now then, we must set to work. 'Tis a good thing ye have the parents coming to live under your roof. I've draped the house with positive energy and good intentions, but 'tis not enough. Where are the amulet and ring?"

"Sage has them. Why?"

"Well, we need them over here to keep an eye on them and keep them completely protected. Agnes always swore she'd have the amulet and ring for herself. She just couldn't find them after your mam packaged them up more than forty years ago. She'd sent them over from Ireland to your Aunt Shannon in Winnipeg. That was a brilliant move on your mam's part, I must say! Removing and hiding them right out of the country, keeping them safe for ye and Keenan."

"Aye. Well, after forty years, it was certainly a surprise for Keenan and me to find out they even existed. Anyway, I can go get them, straight off."

"Aye, 'twould probably be best. When are they planning to move in?"

"Next week."

"Can ye maybe suggest they come a mite sooner, the quicker they are here the better."

"Aye. I'll talk to them today."

"Grand. Now, I'd be thinkin' 'twould be best if we kept this between the pair of us, at least for now. The more people that know will only be giving Agnes power through thought. Kinda' like the law of attraction."

"Aye. Good plan." Tessy grabbed her keys and ran out the door.

On the way over to Sage's she tried to think of a believable excuse to take the amulet and ring. She decided to tell Sage she needed them for a special ritual, and she needed them until after the next full moon. By that time, they would all be living at Ashling Manor.

Much to Tessy's relief Sage bought her story and gladly surrendered the amulet and ring. Tessy stayed for a little while making sure Sage was fine. She managed to slip in the conversation that Sage and Tommy could move in sooner. She mentioned perhaps within the next couple of days.

"Oh, I don't know, Tess. That's awfully soon. We don't want

to be a bother to you and Marshall."

"Bother! Not a bother at all, my dear. Your rooms are ready and just waiting for ye. And, truth be told, you'd be fine company for me with Marshall being gone."

"Well, I suppose. All right then. I'll talk to Tommy tonight and see what he thinks. At least, this way, you wouldn't have to come over here every day."

"Grand, dear. Just grand. All right, love, if you're okay for now, I'll just pop on home and come back a little later to check on ye."

By the time Tessy returned to Ashling Manor she had regained her confidence. She was ready to take on the world, or in this case, the world beyond. She decided that using the amulet and ring in an actual ritual wouldn't be a bad idea. That way, she wouldn't be lying to Sage, either.

She opened the door and called out, "Nilrem! I'm back. I've got them." She went from room to room searching for him, calling out his name. He was nowhere to be found.

"Gone," she said to Merlin, who had followed her around the house.

Tessy took the amulet and ring into the dining room. She opened the china cabinet door and stood looking for just the right vessel for her ritual. She chose a beautiful crystal bowl. It was wide rimmed and shallow. She left it and the amulet and ring on the dining room table and went to her herbal kitchen. She needed to surround the amulet and ring with protective and positive ingredients. She perused through her jars and sacks and picked out just the right herbs, oils, and crystals.

Tessy pulled down a basket and filled it up. She took the basket into the dining room and started by placing a large white pillar candle in the centre of the crystal bowl. Then she placed the herbs around it. There was nettle, wood betony, rosemary, sage, and sea salt for protection. She also added lavender, chamomile and rose petals for peace and harmony. Then she dropped in some black currants and red clover to drive out and remove negative energy. On top of the herbs, she placed the amulet and ring, then arranged a number of protective crystals around them: amethyst, amber, bloodstone, carnelian, smoky quartz, and tiger's eye. She completed the combination by sprinkling a little patchouli, rue, and rosemary essential oils for extra protection.

Tessy quieted and lit the candle. She took in a few deep breaths then chanted:

With these herbs, gems, and oils
I ask to keep away all curses, evils, and spoils.
Protect this ancient amulet and ring
Let only things positive they do bring.
When the time is right for them to shine,
To show their power to keep things in line.
May all those present and under this roof
Stay safe and protected as their proof.
So, banish the evil and make it flee
For this is my will – so mote it be!

Tessy turned and took one more look before she left the room. Whatever was meant to be was now set into motion.

Two days after Tessy's visit, Sage and Tommy moved into Ashling Manor as planned. Sage was set up in the den and Tommy in one of the upstairs guest rooms. Tessy felt quite relieved to have them under her roof where she could keep close tabs on Sage. She hadn't seen hide nor hair of Nilrem since their first encounter, but she was pretty sure he wasn't too far off.

26
Roommates

The phone rang as Tessy came through the back porch door. Sage was resting. Tessy ran as quickly as possible with her boots on.

"Aye. Hello, hello."

"Tessy? It's Dotty. Where did I get you from?"

"Oh, Dotty, dear. Just coming in the door, 'tis all. Is everything all right? Has something happened to Marshall?"

"No. No. Everything here is fine. Marshall and Bert are down at the hardware store picking up a few things."

"Oh, thank goodness."

"Sorry, didn't mean to worry you. I was just wondering if you'd be willing to give up your Guinness stew recipe. Bert and I are having a few people in for St. Patrick's Day next week and your stew is the best I've ever tasted."

"Well, thank ye, dear. Of course, you can have it. I'll pull it up on the computer and send a copy to ye, straight off."

"Thank you, that would be wonderful. And, if you don't mind, maybe a copy of your Irish soda bread, as well."

Tessy chuckled. "Of course, love. So, how are ye and Bert making out living with all the renovations and whatnot?"

"Well, I never in a thousand years expected there to be so much red tape. My oh my. The forms, the restrictions, the guidelines, well, they just go on and on and on. Poor Dr. Tayse. And, the house, I'm sure you wouldn't even recognize it now."

"Aye. I do know poor Marshall has been dealing with a lot, especially, with the legalities of late. There are times I wish I had never suggested it. And I'm sure he does, too." Tessy tittered. "Are ye and Bert still wanting to take over and manage the B&B?"

"Oh yes. Once we get things all straightened out, we are really looking forward to it. To be honest, it's always been a dream of ours. Of course, we were thinking of someplace maybe a little more exotic than Winnipeg." Dotty laughed then continued, "But there are lots of people coming here from all different parts of the world and that's what will make it exciting."

"'Tis going to be a lot of work for ye two."

"Yes. Well, you know how I love to fuss. I believe you've told me that a time or two." Dotty chortled.

"Aye, maybe just a time or two." Tessy teased.

The ladies chatted on for a while longer before Dotty mentioned the contractor had just walked in the door and she needed to show him a few things. Before they hung up, Tessy asked Dotty if she would get Marshall to give her a quick call when he got in. She then wished her well, saying she would send off the recipes straight away and hung up.

As Tessy made her way to the library to turn on the computer, she thought about her Irish stew and St. Patrick's Day. She decided to cancel her usual St. Paddy's shenanigans this year. She hadn't made a big fuss about it because she didn't want Sage to feel responsible in any way. It was just better to let it go this year. No regrets.

About an hour later the phone rang. Tessy checked the call display to see that it was Marshall.

"Hello, love," she answered.

"Hi, darling. Dotty said you wanted me to call. Are you all right? Is everything okay?"

"Aye, love. I'm just fine. How are ye doing? How's the paperwork coming?"

"Good. Yep, the paperwork is all done and ready for the final stamp of approval. I think Dotty, Bert and I are going out to celebrate tonight."

"Oh, Marshall! That's grand news. Congratulations. I wish I was there to help ye celebrate."

"Me too. I miss you. So, what's up?"

"Oh, almost forgot. Just thought I'd let you know you're coming home to a pair of roommates."

"Ah, so it's happened, has it?" He jested. "How's it going?"

"Grand. They're wonderful company. And the sleeping arrangements are working out nicely. Sage is already looking healthier. I think she is sleeping better, too."

"Well, that's great news. I'll book my flight for the day after tomorrow. Can't wait to see everyone. Say hi for me."

"Aye, love. I will. Have a grand time tonight and a safe trip home. See you soon, dear. Bye, for now."

* * *

Marshall pulled into the lane and looked at Ashling Manor in a new light. It was a nice feeling to be coming home to a family again. He smiled. He was even more delighted when Emma and Becky greeted him at the door.

"Grandpa!" they both chimed. Becky had adopted Marshall as her grandpa long ago. Since Dr. Kyle popped the question and is marrying her mom, he will be her fulltime daddy, so now it's official. Becky made that a well-known fact.

The two little girls ran to the foyer for hugs. "Grandpa, Sage and Tommy live here now, too!" Emma duly reported.

"They do? Well, isn't that nice." Marshall beamed.

"Yes. But Sage can't climb stairs because of the babies so she sleeps in the den. But she's in here right now." Emma grabbed Grandpa's hand guiding him into the living room.

"Is that so?" he answered.

"Yes. We've been playing Old Maid with Sage and keeping her company." Becky pointed at the cards scattered on the coffee table.

Sage lay on the couch. She smiled up at Marshall. "Hi. Welcome home. Sorry you've come home to a big lump laying on your couch." She laughed.

"Not at all. It's nice to have you here. How are you feeling?"

"Other than fat and a little uncomfortable, pretty good. Thanks."

"That's good to hear. Hope we can keep it that way. Where's Tess?"

"Oh, she ran out to pick up a couple of things. She should

be back any minute."

"Oh, okay. Well, if you'll excuse me, I'll just head upstairs and start unpacking."

"You bet. I'll send Tessy up when she comes in."

"Great. Thanks. Well then, see you in a bit, roomy!" Marshall teased.

Sage gave a little snicker. "Yep. See ya, roomy."

Marshall was still unpacking when Tessy got home.

She ran up to the bedroom. "Marshall, love. I'm so glad you're home." She gave him a big hug and a kiss. "Sorry I wasn't home to greet ye."

"No problem. It was really nice to come home and be greeted by the kids, though."

"I thought you might like that." Tessy chuckled.

"Yah. Having the house full is going to be kinda different but I think a really good kinda different." Marshall wrapped his arms around Tessy a little tighter. "And, I will have my very own mechanic living right under our roof. Bonus!" Marshall's boyish grin exploded. Tessy laughed.

* * *

Sage was able to get around on the main floor without too much trouble. However, there was only a half bath so when she wanted to shower she needed Tommy to all but carry her upstairs. She stood at the bottom of the stairs looking up the steps to the first landing and the next set that followed to the top. She puffed, "I wish there was an easier way." She looked at her husband.

"Ah, come on. We've got this." Tommy wrapped his arm around her. "We'll just take it slow and easy."

An hour later Sage was sitting at the kitchen table damp-haired, clean and fresh. After Tommy got her back downstairs, he went out to the shop to help Marshall work on the car. Tessy stood over the stove making sure her pot of rice didn't boil over. One of Sage's newest cravings was Tessy's rice pudding.

Sage laughed. "Between you spoiling me and Tommy getting to spend all his time out in that shop working on Brigid, we are never going to want to leave. Thank you so much for everything, Tessy. We really do appreciate all you and Marshall are doing."

"We love having you here, my dear. You've been grand company. I just hope you're comfortable enough in the den."

"Oh yes. Very. In fact, I've had fewer bad dreams since I've been here. I've been sleeping like a baby."

"Ah, that's grand to hear." Tessy looked up toward the ceiling and smiled. *Thank ye, Nilrem.*

* * *

Dotty's phone call got Tessy longing for her Guinness stew. Just because she wasn't throwing her St. Paddy's celebration didn't mean they couldn't enjoy a fine Irish stew. She ran down to Kessel's Grocery the day before the 17th and picked up all the ingredients to make the stew and Irish soda bread. The next morning, she pulled out the crockpot and created the magickal stew. The delicious smells permeated through the house all day. By suppertime, everyone's appetite was ferocious. It did Tessy's heart good to see her loved ones enjoying her labours. It was especially satisfying to see Sage with such a healthy appetite. She wondered about Nilrem and decided she would try to secretly leave him a bowl full after everyone retired for the night.

* * *

Tessy felt Nilrem's calming presence but had not encountered him since his first appearance. However, the bowl of stew she left out had been cleaned up and mysteriously put back in the cupboard by morning.

Like Sage, her bad dreams had subsided somewhat. She credited it to Nilrem's presence. She'd incorporated a dream catcher and a large amethyst in both the den and her bedroom to help protect them from recurrent nightmares. Even with Nilrem's calming powers, she thought it certainly couldn't hurt.

27
Family

It was Ostara or what most call Spring Equinox. Sage was just over thirty weeks pregnant. Time was ticking and even though Dr. Kyle predicted an early delivery, it wasn't ticking fast enough for Sage.

There had been some beautiful sunny days that made the snow sticky and wet. It was perfect for building a handsome snowman. Sage, feeling quite housebound, stood at the window, and watched Emma and Becky do just that.

Tommy had ventured out with a hat, scarf, and mitts to adorn their snowy creation. He got so caught up in the fun, he convinced them that Mr. Snowman needed a Mrs. Snowwoman. Sage laughed at her husband's delightful childlike involvement.

Tessy heard Sage's laughter and went to investigate. Soon, she too was giggling at the snow day shenanigans.

"He really is going to make a great dad, isn't he?" Sage lovingly boasted.

"Aye. He certainly is. Never had a doubt, my dear. Those wee poppets are going to be very blessed to have parents such as ye two."

"Thanks, Tessy. We're sure going to try." Sage glanced down and rubbed her belly. She looked back out the window in time to see a snowball fight erupt. It looked like Tommy was getting the brunt of it. The dogs were intercepting most of his snowballs. She and Tessy both let out a hearty laugh.

When Tommy and the girls finished Mrs. Snowwoman they decided to come in for hot chocolate. The girls stripped off their wet clothes and made their way to the kitchen. They had worn snow pants, but Tommy had to go upstairs and change into some dry blue jeans.

Tommy loved being part of this large family. He grew up as an only child. It was just him and his mom. When his mom died, he had no one. He counted his blessings every day that he somehow landed where he did. His new beginnings in Ladyslipper were life changing. And soon he would be the father of twins. He was so happy to know his children would never be alone. When he returned downstairs, he stood at the kitchen door. There at the table sat people he loved, people who loved him.

Emma and Becky were telling Grandpa all about their snowy fun.

"Yep. We made Mr. Snowman first and then Tommy thought we should make a Mrs. for him so he wouldn't be lonely. Wasn't that a good idea?" Emma merrily chattered between sips.

"Really? Well, yes. That was a good idea. I'll have to go out and take a look when we're finished our hot chocolate."

"Yes," the girls squealed.

Tommy walked behind the girls and tousled their hair on the way by. "Nice hair," he teased.

"Hey!" they chimed, trying to smooth down their tuque hair.

Tommy laughed.

Sage piped up, "Tommy! Stop pestering them."

"Hey. Did you see how they hammered me with snowballs?"

"Oh yah, Grandpa. You shoulda seen. We got him good." Emma buckled with laughter.

Marshall looked at Tommy and laughed. Then he congratulated the girls. "Nice job. Wished I'd seen that."

Tommy shook his head and beamed at everyone.

The little girls left when they finished their hot chocolate. As promised, Marshall went out with the girls to inspect their snowmen then he and Tommy headed to the shop. Sage went down for a nap and Tessy sat at the table checking through her orders. It was so quiet she could hear the clock ticking. She looked down at the dogs, who were also napping. "'Tis been a while since it's been this peaceful around here," she mused.

Tessy's tranquil moment didn't last long. She heard a commotion at the back door. With a quick knock, Sarah and Cherokee let themselves in.

"Hey," they greeted.

"Well, hello, my dears. Come in. Come in." Tessy gathered up her papers and set them off to the side.

"We hope you don't mind but we were wondering if we could get some more magazines and work here on our journals for a while?"

"Not at all. Certainly. How are they coming along? 'Twon't be long before they're due."

"Yes. We know. That's why we're here. They are coming along

pretty good. Wouldn't you say Cherokee?"

"Yep. I've really enjoyed working on mine. I find it's such a peaceful and calming assignment."

"Exactly. Me too."

"Well, that's grand. Glad they're working out for ye. I'm sure you'll both get a fine grade."

"Boy, sure hope so. Well, we'll just head up to the attic, if that's okay?"

"Aye. Just don't be too noisy. Sage is resting."

"Oh. Okay."

By the time Sage got up, Sarah and Cherokee were at the kitchen table cutting and gluing.

"Hey guys." Sage chirped as she waddled into the kitchen.

Sarah was closest and jumped up to pull out a chair for her. "Hey. How are you feeling?"

"Oh, big as a house, but fine, thanks." She laughed. "Tessy and Marshall have been spoiling us rotten."

"I can only imagine," Cherokee said. "But, hey, that's a good thing."

Everyone laughed.

Sage eased herself down onto the chair. She looked over at the scrapbooks the girls were working on. "So, how are your career journals coming along?"

"Great," Cherokee said. "We were just telling Tessy how much we've enjoyed working on them. But I'm still glad we're almost done."

"Yah." Sarah groaned. "I think the hardest thing about this

whole project will be writing the essay that has to go with it."

Tessy stood at the sink and looked over. "Have you girls discovered any distinct career decisions while working on your journals?"

Sarah thought for a moment. "Actually, yes. Other than both of us taking the basic practical herbalist course, we are heading in different directions."

"Oh, like what?" Sage was excited.

"Well, I've decided on courses like fermentation, herb-drug-nutrient interaction, nutrition and iridology."

"And I'm heading towards master herbalist and shamanic practitioner," Cherokee said. "It'll take a few more years, but I think it'll be worth it in the long run."

"Wow. Great courses you guys. I'm impressed. Iridology is being able to tell someone's health by studying the iris of the eye, right Sarah?"

"Yes, I can't wait to start that course." Sarah gave a wide-mouth grin.

Tessy added, "I can see why each of you girls have chosen those particular paths. Sarah, you originally wanted to go into nursing and Cherokee, your cultural and educational background are your foundation. I know you will both succeed beyond our wildest dreams. I couldn't be prouder."

"Thanks. I know we're sure going to try our best, right Sarah?" Cherokee looked over at her friend.

"Absolutely. We're pretty stoked." Sarah reached over and knuckle bumped her best friend.

"I bet." Sage laughed.

Tommy walked in just in time to see the girls laughing. Once again, the table was full of people he loved. *Family,* he smiled to himself. There were no words for the overwhelming feeling of joy and belonging. He only hoped, somehow, his mom was watching from beyond.

28
Laying the Groundwork

It was the darkest part of the night. Those mystical moments before the light of dawn seeps across the sky. Tessy's dream found her in a field of herbs, the scent deliciously intoxicating. The sun warmed her face and the sound of the bumblebees mesmerized her. It was a vision of leisure and enchantment. *Find the clan named after the herbs* spilled into Tessy's mind. Suddenly there was the familiar and haunting cackle of Agnes's evil laughter ringing in her ears.

Tessy woke with a start. She instantly sat up and scanned the room to ensure Agnes was nowhere to be seen. She looked over at Marshall. He snored contently. Tessy rose from bed, a little shaky. She put on her housecoat and went straight down to the den to check on Sage. She quietly slid open the pocket door and peeked in. Sage was asleep. She stuck her head in a little farther to make sure there were no unwanted auras about the room. It was all clear. Tessy closed the door and went to the kitchen to make some warm milk and honey to calm down. She stood at the stove blankly staring into the pot. *I need to get a clear understanding of how I can protect Sage and the babies and still get Agnes to peacefully crossover.* She heard something stir behind her. Tessy immediately placed a dome of white light over her and spun around. Silent purple sparks burst throughout the room.

It was Nilrem.

"Leapin' Leprechauns, Nilrem! What are ye doin' sneaking up on me in the middle of the night? You've 'bout scared ten years off me life."

Nilrem chuckled. "Sorry Tess. I was comin' to check on ye, is all. And, to see what ye are plannin' to do about Agnes."

"Don't you mean what we're plannin' to do about Agnes?" Tessy asked.

"Well lass, bein' of a different realm there is only so much I can help ye with. Other than passin' on what information I have acquired and drapin' positive energy, there is little else I can do until she surfaces."

"I thought ye said between the pair of us, we could stop her in her tracks?"

"Aye. Once she surfaces, I can do a mite more from this side."

"Oh, that's just grand! Well, I guess I best be doin' a little research then." Tessy puffed. She turned off the burner. "Would ye care to join me in a cup of milk and honey?"

"Nye, thanks. I just came to check on ye. I'll be headin' off, now. I shan't be far if ye need me. Good night to ye. Oh! Don't be forgettin' the power of the amulet and ring!" And with that, he was gone as quick and unusually silent as his arrival.

Tessy still didn't know where he flashed in from or popped off to. She was, however, very thankful she had an elemental ally to count on for this nightmarish ordeal. *I wonder what he meant about the power of the amulet and ring.*

Tessy sipped on her hot milk and honey and decided to make a trip up to the attic. It had been many years since she was forced to use this kind of magick and needed to brush up on a few things. It was plain to see that she was not going to get back to sleep. She might as well do something constructive while she was up. She picked up her cup and off she went.

As quietly as possible she wiggled and popped the attic door open and climbed the stairs. She did her best to manoeuvre around any memorized creaks on the steps. On the far side of the attic was her sacred trunk. She got the key from its hiding spot and stood over the vessel of wonder. She pulled over a nearby crate and sat down. She inserted the key and heard the lock click into place. As she opened it, the curved lid groaned from lack of use. Tessy lifted out a few miscellaneous magickal tools and set them aside. There it was, her grimoire.

This sacred journal was handed down through the centuries. As a child, Tessy remembered witnessing her granny, shortly before her death, hand the grimoire to her mother. Her mother, in turn, passed it on to Tessy when she turned sixteen. That was just weeks before her parents' fatal car accident. She reverently laid the large leather-cased book on her lap and gently placed her hand on it. She closed her eyes. She could feel the power of the book rumbling and vibrating. The tattered and yellowed pages permeated healing and other ancient spell castings, chants, and recipes. She was honoured to be in possession of such history. She held the highest regard for the maidens, mothers and crones that came before her, sharing their knowledge and secrets. Some to the degree of facing their death, judged, condemned, and punished out of fear and ignorance.

Tessy lifted her hand from the book and shook off the trance. She needed to get down to business. She didn't really want to take the book downstairs for fear of having it exposed but the lighting in the attic was near impossible to read by. The trunk had all the tools and ingredients she would require but for now she placed the stray items back in and closed the lid. She cradled the book under one arm, picked up her milk and tiptoed back downstairs into the library.

Tessy closed the door, placed her milk and the heavy book onto the mahogany desk and switched on the banker's lamp. When she unfastened the leather strap the book flopped open with a thud. It was as if the binding safely held the magick within. The smell of age and herbs burst up into Tessy's senses almost knocking her head back. Tears sprang to her eyes, and it took a moment for her to focus. As she gently turned the tattered sheets she smiled. She was reminded how her ancestors had tucked away different tools and ingredients within the hallowed pages. There were feathers, long stemmed flowers, herbs, pieces of coloured fabric, locks of hair, strands of string and ribbons, along with pressed moths, drips of candle wax, and drops of blood from a carefully pricked finger. They were all intertwined with chants and the recipes that went with them. Tessy searched for a spell that would provide a bit more clout than lovely flowers and locks of hair. She needed something quite terrifying, and she knew, with a little research, she would find just the right spell to do the trick.

There was only one other time she summoned a similar spell many, many years ago. She had never forgotten what both her mother and granny cautioned her about conjuring up such magick.

Before ye summon anything ye best be makin' darn sure ye know how to banish it.

That lesson always haunted Tessy, just a bit.

The last time she used such a spell was when she was a university student in Winnipeg. Her best friend at the time had been dating a fellow and after showing his true colours she broke up with him. He stalked her, terrified her, and eventually beat her so badly that Tessy didn't recognise her when she went to visit her in the hospital. There is nothing more dangerous or powerful than an enraged enchantress! That was exactly what Tessy was. She lured that creep into a quiet, secluded park. Then she conjured up the most hideous monster possible and scared him so badly he never stalked or touched another woman in violence ever again. That was the type of spell Tessy needed now. She had turned into a momma bear. Her darling Sage and her wee babes were in grave danger. Tessy wasn't fooling around with any light-hearted bibbity-bobbity-boo stuff. She didn't think she needed anything quite that drastic but something convincing enough to make sure Agnes turned to the light and went home for good, never to return.

Tessy forgot how the book pulled you into the very realm of the magickal antiquity. How the pages mesmerized and consumed your very soul. The minutes turned into hours. Tessy heard some rustling in the kitchen and drifted back to reality. She was shocked when she looked at the clock. She'd been engrossed in her research for over three hours. She slowly stood and stretched her neck and back while reaching her arms high into the air, then glanced around for a good hiding spot for the grimoire. She decided the bottom cupboard of the credenza. It barely fit but that would have to work, for now.

She made her way to the kitchen and smelled the coffee brewing. She turned the corner and there was Tommy in his sleep pants and T-shirt shuffling around in his slippers. He was getting down cups, plates, and cutlery for everyone.

What a sweet boy, he is, she thought. "Mornin' to ye, Tommy dear."

"Oh, mornin' Tess!" Tommy greeted. "I saw that you were up when I went past your room but didn't know where you were."

"Oh sorry, dear. I was in the library doing a little research. I should have had coffee on for ye, but the time got away on me."

"No problem. You are not here to wait on us. It's so nice of you to let us stay while Sage is kinda bedridden."

"Nonsense! I wouldn't have it any other way. You and Sage are family and that's what family does. You'll not be going anywhere anytime soon. Even after the wee babes are born."

"Oh Tessy, I don't know about that. We don't want to impose on you and Marshall any more than we already have. And, after they're born, the babies will be up and crying night and day. We can't do that to you."

"Ye most certainly can. We are here to help ye in any way we can and will. A house this size is meant to be filled with family."

"Well, thanks Tess. But we'll see how it goes. Coffee?" Tommy held up the coffee pot.

"Aye, I could certainly use a cup or two this morning." Tessy sighed.

"Something wrong, Tess?" Tommy looked concerned as he pulled out a chair to sit at the table.

Tessy was sorry she let her concerns slip out. Sage and Tommy didn't need anything else to worry about. "Oh no, dear. I just didn't sleep well last night, 'tis all. Thanks. Nothing that a good afternoon nap won't cure." She chuckled.

"That's good. Well, I'll be at work and Sage sleeps a lot of the time so you should be able to take that nap without too many disturbances." Tommy held up his cup to her. "I've got to go get ready, so I'll just take this upstairs. See you later." And off he went.

Tessy took in a long breath as she gazed deep into the dark brew in her cup. She was tired from her restless night but needed to keep going. As she stared into her cup the coffee started to swirl and an image appeared. She looked deeper. It was an image of the amulet and the ring.

"That's it. That's what Nilrem meant." Tessy gasped out loud. She left her coffee and ran to the dining room where the amulet and ring were still resting in the protective herb mixture. She gazed down at them.

Somehow, she had to get Sage and Tommy to wear these

and not take them off until the danger was over, and Agnes was securely transported to the otherworld.

29
Spilling the Beans

Tessy was up early every morning for the next week, diving deep into the depths of the sacred journal. She researched and copied down ancient secrets of power and wisdom. She then spent the day assembling, concocting, and distributing compounds of protection and positive energy throughout the house. She tried to be as nonchalant and unassuming as possible. Apparently, she was not that triumphant at it.

Marshall noticed more and more crystals popping up around the house. There were a number of candles burning with strange symbols carved on them and bowls of herbs were everywhere. One morning when he and Tessy were alone in the kitchen, he couldn't stay silent.

"Darling, you probably think I usually have no idea what's going on around here, and most of the time you'd be right. But even I know something is brewing. So, what's the scoop?"

Tessy was afraid this would happen. She wasn't sure how much to divulge or even where to begin. But Marshall had a right to know. She took Marshall by the hand, lead him down the hall and out to the front veranda so not to be overheard. The spring sunshine was strong and warm enough for them to sit out for a few minutes without coats. They sat close on the wicker loveseat. Still holding his hand, she looked up into his blue eyes.

"'Tis Agnes."

"Agnes!" Marshall blurted. "She's dead."

"Aye. Yes and no."

"Tessy. Seriously. Give me a break."

"I know. I know, love. I thought the same when Nilrem told me."

"Nilrem? Who the hell is Nilrem?"

Tessy chuckled. "Well, remember the odd little shopkeeper we encountered in Kilkenny?"

"Yes?"

"That's Nilrem."

"What? How? What?"

Tessy pat Marshall on the chest. "Just hear me out, love. Ye see, Nilrem isn't quite of this world. He apparently has been one of my guardians since birth. He followed us throughout Ireland keeping an eye on us while we were investigating Agnes. I saw glimpses of him in Ireland but only just met him recently. He came to warn me that Agnes did not cross over and wants to steal Sage's babies."

"What? Oh Tess, this is all a little much."

"I know, love. I agree. I'm sorry. But I feel 'tis true. Ye know how Sage and I have been having terrible dreams of late?"

"Yes. Do they have something to do with all this?"

"Aye. I believe so. 'Tis Agnes haunting us. It's like what you would understand to be a poltergeist affect."

"Well, how the hell do you fight a ghost?"

"That's what I'm working on, love."

As it turned out, Marshall wasn't the only one that took note of all the extra precautions around the house. Sage was also curious.

"Tess? If you put one more crystal in my room, I won't be able to move." She laughed. I've also noticed you've got herbs hanging over every door and every window throughout the house. I know this isn't all for Ostara. You've taught me well enough to recognize something's going on. Spill the beans."

Tessy took a deep breath. How, on God's green earth, was she going to tell Sage without scaring her half to death? She got Sage comfortably seated in the living room. She sat close and held her hand. Tessy managed to get the whole story out and still keep Sage's level of terror to a minimum. It certainly helped that Tessy had been grooming Sage for the last year. Tessy finished the conversation with, "I vow to ye, nothing will harm ye or those wee babes."

Tessy went to the library, got the grimoire, and returned to the living room. She sat with Sage and shared her most sacred possession. After all, one day this priceless piece of history would be handed over to the next generation of a gifted Haggertys, and that was Sage.

For the next hour the two of them faced this paranormal predicament with their combined knowledge of magickal wisdom and spiritual understanding. Even though Sage was frightened she looked forward to putting into practice all the lessons she had absorbed over the past year.

Tessy was astonished at how well Sage was handling

everything. Her true Celtic heritage shone like a beacon. For now, at least, they agreed it best not to share any of this with Tommy.

Tessy was relieved the cat was out of the bag and she had another ally in fighting this demon. Now she didn't have to worry about where or when Nilrem popped up. She wondered about calling him in and introducing him to Sage. Then she thought it best to wait. When the time was right it would happen.

Tessy noticed Sage proudly wearing the amulet, however, she knew getting Tommy to wear the ring would be a bit of a challenge. Especially, when Tommy worked with his hands all day. Both she and Sage needed to put their thinking caps on to solve the problem.

Sage was in the kitchen having her tea when she called out. "Tessy. Tessy." She waddled her way out of the kitchen to find Tessy as quickly as possible.

"Aye, dear. What is it?" Tessy came running out the library door and met Sage in the hallway.

"I'm fine. Sorry, didn't mean to scare you. I think I've found a way for Tommy to wear the ring." Sage beamed.

"Wonderful. What do ye have in mind?"

"What if I convinced him to wear it around his neck on a chain under his shirt? Would the ring still have its power?"

"Aye. I'd think 'twould work just fine."

"Great, but I don't have a chain that would work for a guy." Sage winced.

"Oh, don't ye mind. I've got plenty of chains upstairs. One

176

of them will be bound to work. I'll go fetch my jewellery box and bring it down so we can go through it."

Tessy smiled as she headed upstairs. Another problem solved.

30
Lessons in Empathy and Angels

Part of Tessy's research included finding out as much as she could about Agnes. While in Ireland, she and her brother, Keenan discovered some interesting facts about her. However, those elements mostly had to do with the death of their parents, Garret and Teagan O'Conner. Tessy needed to delve into the depths of who Agnes really was and how she ended up the way she did. Then, hopefully, she could get a better understanding of how to deal with her.

Tessy knew she needed to talk to her older cousin Marie, in Ireland. Marie had more information about Agnes than anyone. There was no time to waste. Tessy decided a surprise phone call would have to take precedence over a detailed letter. Tessy looked at the clock. It was just after eight in the morning. That would make it mid-afternoon in Ireland. She walked over to her writing desk and pulled out her address book. She dialled the long list of numbers. It rang a few times. Just as Tessy was about to hang up, Marie answered. "Good day! Good day, to ye!" she puffed into the phone.

"Marie, love? Is that ye?" Tessy spoke loudly into the phone.

"Aye. Who's this, then?"

"Marie, dear, 'tis cousin Tessy."

"Well, Tessy, as I live and breathe. How grand to hear your

voice, dear. What are ye doin' callin' me in the middle of the day?"

Tessy smiled and shook her head. She never had to wonder what was on Marie's mind. "Grand to hear ye, as well. I'm needin' your help with some more information 'bout Agnes."

"Agnes! Why on God's green pastures would ye be wantin' any more information 'bout Aggie? Good riddance to her, I'd say."

"Well love, I really can't go into any details right now, but there are some things I must know. Please."

Tessy had a list of very specific questions she needed answered. Marie did her best to answer every single one. By time they hung up, Tessy felt she had a pretty good idea as to why Agnes ended up in an institution.

Agnes Haggerty's family history was not a happy one. Her parents were both heavy drinkers. Agnes, being the oldest daughter of a large poverty-stricken family, was often neglected and left to raise her younger siblings. She had five brothers, three of which were older and gone most of the time. The remaining two brothers and four sisters, two of which were twins depended heavily on Agnes. Unfortunately, the twins died very young in a house fire. Agnes was alone with them when the fire broke out. At the age of barely thirteen, she returned into the burning inferno over and over again trying to get everyone out. She was unable to reach the two wee ones and they perished. She never forgave herself and neither did her family. Agnes was shunned. By the age of sixteen she was living on her own and periodically institutionalized off and on from that time until her death.

When Tessy and Keenan finally tracked Agnes down in Ireland she was in a mental institution in Dublin. An appalling childhood was not the only memory Agnes struggled with.

She was in love with Tessy's father, Garret, and wanted Tessy's mother, Teagan, out of the way. Then she believed she could have him, the twins, and the amulet and ring, all for herself. To her great dismay, her plan backfired. Both Garret and Teagan died in the horrific car crash she had planned solely for Teagan. Even though Agnes had murdered her parents forty years earlier, Tessy felt only pity and compassion for Agnes as she lay on her deathbed a year ago, old and mentally tortured.

After falling privy to the most recent information about Agnes, Tessy's compassion for her greatly increased to a depth of true heartache. Now, more than ever, her desire to get Agnes to peacefully crossover was immeasurable. Her poor tortured soul deserved to finally be at rest.

* * *

Sage convinced Tommy to wear the ring around his neck by telling him it was an ancient Haggerty tradition. The husband must wear the ring during the last weeks of pregnancy to ensure a safe delivery. She figured that was as close to the truth as possible. Tommy was more than eager to do his small part and complied.

"Bless his soul," Tessy said when Sage told her. "What a sweet lad he is. Well, it will help our fight."

Sage sat at the kitchen table while Tessy tidied up after breakfast. Tommy was at work and Marshall was out in the shop waiting for his grandson, Matt, and his friends.

"Tessy, what will happen to Agnes?" Sage asked.

"Well, hopefully, we'll get her to move into the light."

"How are we going to do that?"

"I haven't got all the details worked out just yet. I must talk to Nilrem, but I'm hoping to trap her in a sort of vortex."

"A vortex," Sage exclaimed.

Tessy chuckled. "Aye. As I said, I haven't got it all worked out yet."

"Why would she go to the light now when she didn't before?"

"I'll be calling on some pretty powerful angels and assistants." Tessy smiled.

"Angels? But Agnes is pure evil. Why would the angels help her?"

"Agnes has a troubled, tortured soul. If we can convince her to cross over into the light, her soul could then be cocooned and healed."

"Cocooned? What's that?"

Tessy laughed and sat down beside Sage. "Cocooning happens when a tortured or a horribly traumatized soul returns to the Otherside. It arrives tired, broken, and sometimes in shock. It needs to rest and heal. The spirit is wrapped in God's pure loving energy and remains cocooned for as long as it takes to become healthy and whole again. Hopefully, that is what will happen to Agnes's soul."

"But why would you even care if she crosses over?" Sage asked. "She killed your parents and wants to steal my babies."

"We must always try to hold forgiveness in our hearts, so we don't become as tainted and hateful as the sick and tortured. 'Tis not always easy, I'll agree. We also don't want her to ever return." Tessy patted Sage's hand.

"Well, all I know is I want her gone. I don't care where or how. Just gone. She's terrifying!"

"Aye, she is. That's why when she shows up, and she will, we'll have to start by calling in creatures just as terrifying. The only way to catch her attention is to stoop to a level she understands. We have to persuade her into our battlefield. Then we call in the angels, and all others who want to assist, to hopefully, guide her over."

"Ooh, what do you have in mind?" Sage rubbed her hands together.

Tessy laughed. "I'll let ye know in due course. I don't plan on her showing up until after the babies are born. So, we've some time yet to set the scheme into place."

31
Spring Day Outing with Repercussions

With Dr. Kyle's prediction of an early delivery, it meant there were only a couple of weeks, at best, remaining before the big day. Easter was late this year, not until the second last weekend in April. Tessy mused if Sage would hold off long enough to have Easter babies.

She saw a couple of matching bunny sleepers when she was shopping the other day and imagined how cute they would look on the twins. She debated buying them but decided that might alter the date in some way. Not wanting to toy with the Universe, she left them in the store.

* * *

Time was ticking. Tessy needed to collaborate with Nilrem soon in order to execute their united front. She decided the next time she was alone she would summon him.

A few days later, Tessy got her wish. Jim asked Marshall if he'd come down to the pharmacy to help build some new shelving. Sage had her last doctor's appointment before delivery and wanted Tommy there with her. The moment they were all out the door, Tessy headed to the kitchen and called out Nilrem's name. Cracks and pops of purple sparks danced through the air and a faint hue filled the room. At the grand finale, there stood Nilrem.

"Well, top'o'the mornin' to ye!" he greeted.

Tessy chuckled. "My, ye do like to make a grand entrance, ye do."

"Well, what's the point of enterin' a room if nobody knows ye're there?" Nilrem winked.

Tessy laughed and shook her head. "Well, thank ye for coming. We've plenty to talk over."

By the time Sage and Tommy returned home Tessy had orchestrated her plan in great detail to Nilrem. She hoped it wasn't going to be necessary to bring in any overly destructive forces. Tessy realized that the demons in Agnes's own mind were probably more terrifying than anything she could ever conjure up. Tessy was planning on those demons showing up so she could banish them forever. Nilrem was pleased and completely onboard.

* * *

Mid-April had finally arrived in all its splendour. After last week's typical prairie spring weather of a dump of heavy wet snow, it was nice to see the warm sun shining bright. The melted snow ran off the rooftops and the Canada geese noisily announced their arrival. Except for her doctor's appointment, Sage had been housebound for weeks.

"I want to go out for a walk, today!" she demanded as she set her breakfast plate in the sink.

"Oh Babe. I, I, don't know about that." Tommy winced as he looked up from his second helping of pancakes, bacon, and eggs.

"Come on! It's a beautiful Sunday morning. I've been cooped up in the house for weeks and I'm tired of just laying around. I'll be fine," she whined.

"But Dr. Kyle said—" Tommy started.

"Oh, Dr. Kyle! He's way too cautious. I'm not due for a while yet."

"Yes, but he did say you'll be early."

"Come on!" Sage repeated, stomping her foot.

Tommy could tell Sage was adamant and that he was unlikely to win this argument. He looked over to Tessy then Marshall for some backup. "Marshall, you're the doctor, what do you think?" Tommy asked in his last effort to dissuade his wife.

"Well, I can see your concern, but the fresh air certainly wouldn't hurt her any. However, with that being said, I'd advise she take every precaution. There are still lots of icy spots in the shaded areas. So be careful and don't overdo it."

"Thank you, Marshall!" Sage squealed. She waddled up behind Marshall and gave him a big hug. "I'll go get dressed before anyone changes their mind," she added as she left the room.

Sage was dressed and back in the kitchen before Tommy finished breakfast. She sat down beside him and stared at him like a puppy anxiously waiting to go for a walk.

Tommy looked up from his plate and laughed. "Okay. Okay. Let's go." He picked up his dirty dishes and put them in the sink on the way out of the kitchen.

Tessy and Marshall chuckled as they heard Sage and Tommy bantering at one another down to the foyer and out the door. Tessy looked up at her husband. "What a wonderful couple they make."

Marshall wrapped his arms around her. "Yes, they do. Just like another couple I know." He lovingly smiled at his wife and kissed her.

* * *

Sage and Tommy slowly walked hand in hand. The warmth of the spring sun and fresh air felt like heaven to Sage. She took in some deep cleansing breaths. "Oh, this is amazing. I don't ever want to go back inside."

Tommy laughed. "I think you might change your mind in a few hours. Especially if you catch a whiff of Tessy's delicious cooking."

"Just what are you suggesting?"

"Well, you have been eating for three lately." Tommy teased.

"Hey." Sage playfully slapped him. "You just never mind."

Sage couldn't believe how much she enjoyed just being. The sky was bluer than blue. She could sense the trees ready to burst into bud. The birds flitted and flirted with innocence ready to find a mate and start anew.

186

She lovingly placed her hand on her belly.

They walked in silence all the way down the lane and just past the front of the property. Tommy felt Sage's hand tighten. He looked over at his wife. "Are you all right, babe?"

Sage gave him a funny look. "Yah, I think so." Suddenly Sage lost her footing on some of that ice Marshall had cautioned her about. Down she went before Tommy could catch her.

"Sage! Oh, I'm so sorry. Are you okay?"

"I'm not sure." Sage held her belly.

Tommy tried to help her up. "No!" she cried. "Wait! Stop!"

Tommy got down on his knees beside her. "What's wrong?"

"I had a funny pain then I fell. I think my water just broke." Sage gave Tommy a wide-eyed stare.

"Oh my God!" Tommy yelled. "Will you be all right while I run up to the house to get Tessy's car?"

"Yes. I think so. But hurry!" Sage pleaded.

32
Hurry Up and Wait

Distraught, Tommy sat in the waiting room with his head in his hands. Tessy and Marshall hovered nearby. Tessy stepped close and placed her hand on Tommy's back. He looked up.

"It's all my fault. I should have caught her." He moaned.

"Tommy, dear, it's no one's fault. I'm sure she'll be fine."

"I wish Dr. Kyle would just hurry up and tell us what's happening. I need to be with her."

"You know he's very thorough and that he's doing everything he can." Tessy assured.

"Oh, I hope so." Tommy exhaled.

"He's a wonderful doctor," Tessy added.

Marshall was quiet. Tessy could tell he felt a little responsible. "I should have kept my big mouth shut. I'm sorry, Tommy."

Tommy gave Marshall a faint smile. "I asked for your opinion. Everything would have been fine if I hadn't let her fall."

"Didn't Sage say that she felt a pain and that's what made her lose her footing and fall?" Tessy asked.

"Yes," Tommy said.

"Well then, the problem wasn't her falling. I'm thinking her water broke before she went down." Tessy concluded.

"Maybe," Tommy responded in hopeful reflection.

Tommy didn't want to call Sage's mother until he talked

to Dr. Kyle and had something to report. Being so far away in Ontario, he didn't want to frighten Rosemary any more than necessary. He would call as soon as he got to see Sage.

Another twenty-five minutes went by before Dr. Kyle entered the waiting room. He walked straight over to Tommy. They all stood when they saw him approaching.

"How is she?" Tommy blurted.

"She's doing good for now. The sac has ruptured, and the amniotic fluid is slowly leaking. I've put her on IV for hydration and some antibiotics to ward off any infections. We're closely monitoring both her and the babies. She'll remain here until the babies are born." Kyle looked at Tommy. "You can go in and see her now. I'll be right in to talk to both of you."

Tommy dashed down the hall and into Sage's room. Kyle chatted with Tessy and Marshall for a couple of minutes. He wanted to give Tommy and Sage some time alone but soon joined them. Tessy and Marshall continued to wait.

"Well, that's about as good news as we can expect for now," Tessy said, while tightly ringing a hankie into knots.

Marshall sympathetically reached for Tessy's hands. "It's just like you told Tommy, she'll be fine, sweetheart. Kyle is an excellent doctor."

"Aye, that he is." Tessy hadn't mentioned to Marshall she'd called for a little outside assistance. She invoked Archangel Raphael, the powerful healer, and Diana, the goddess of childbirth, particularly twins. It wasn't that she thought Kyle couldn't handle whatever came up, but she felt better knowing all the bases were covered.

A little over an hour later, Tommy returned to the waiting room.

"How is she, love?" Tessy anxiously asked.

"She's pretty tired, so I thought I'd go and let her sleep." Tommy plunked down in the nearest chair.

"Is there anything we can do?" Tessy asked.

"No. Thanks."

"Can I get you a coffee or something?" Marshall offered.

"No. I'm good, thanks."

"Did you call Rosemary while you were with Sage, dear?" Tessy enquired.

"Yes. Sage talked to her and hopefully eased her anxiety a bit."

"Aye. I'm sure she must be just frantic. Poor dear. I'll have to give her a call a little later on."

"She'd probably really appreciate that, Tess. Thanks."

Kyle came back down the hall. "Why don't you all take a break and go home for a while. Maybe get something to eat. Sage is resting comfortably and I'm pretty sure it's going to be at least a day or two before anything happens. If anything changes, I'll let you know right way."

"Oh, I don't know, Doc." Tommy shook his head.

Tessy rested her hand on his shoulder. "Tommy, dear. There's nothing ye can do right at the moment. Come home with us. I'll make a nice supper and ye can come back later this evening."

Dr. Kyle smiled. "You're going to have to keep up your

strength, Tommy. You are about to have twins. We don't want you taking up a bed in here, too." He teased, trying to lighten the mood.

"Well, okay. But, if anything, and I mean anything, changes you let me know right away."

"You bet." Kyle slapped Tommy on the back. "Well, I have to make some rounds. Catch you all later." And with that, he turned and left.

* * *

The next twenty-four hours were excruciating for Tommy, and he practically lived at the hospital. For the most part, Sage was comfortable and in good spirits. She seemed to be doing much better than her husband.

"Tommy, I'm in good hands," she assured him. "Everyone here has been wonderful and they're keeping really close tabs on me and the babies. I think you should go to work for a while. I know this is a busy time for you with all the farmers getting their machinery ready for seeding."

"Wow. Look at you, sounding like a real farm mechanic's wife." Tommy chuckled.

"I've been paying attention. It may have taken a couple of years, but I think I'm finally catching on." Sage spoke with a playful manner of confidence and her nose high in the air.

"Well, the guys have been really good at covering for me, but I know they are swamped. If you're sure you don't mind maybe

I will go and check on how they're doing. Tessy said she'd be in to see you this morning. Oh, she called your mom last night and they had a good talk. I think Tessy really helped calm her. I'm sure she'll tell you all about it when she gets here. And, if you need anything I'm sure she'll gladly get whatever you need."

"Oh great! I'm so happy to hear she called Mom. Now, I think it's a great idea that you go to work. So … go, get out of here for a while."

"Okay, but if you need me for anything, you text me right away," Tommy insisted.

"Yes, dear. Go!" Sage giggled.

Tommy leaned over, kissed his wife, and headed off to work.

33
Precious Bundles from Heaven

Thirty-one hours later, Tessy and Marshall stood in the presence of two beaming parents, each cradling a precious bundle. Tessy stepped closer and peeked at the wee darling Sage held. Sage pulled the receiving blanket away from the tiny face and proudly announced, "I'd like you to meet Willow Rose Haggerty Bracken."

Teary-eyed Tessy cooed, "Ah, wee Willow Rose. Rose, after your grandmother. How special."

Tommy moved close and made the next introduction. "This is our youngest, Poppy June, June, after my mother. I sure wish she was here to see them."

"Tommy dear, know that she is here and loving them as much as if she stood right before ye."

Tessy couldn't help but let the happy tears spill. She took out a hankie and dabbed her eyes and nose. "Oh, blessed be! Two sweet wee angels." Then she silently thanked God, Raphael, and Diana for their assistance.

Tommy handed Poppy to Tessy while Sage lifted Willow up into Marshall's arms. After holding her for a minute, Marshall smiled down at Sage. "She's a good size for a preemie."

"Yes. They both are. Poppy is a little smaller, but Dr. Kyle said she's doing just fine."

* * *

Sage went home two days after the delivery, but Dr. Kyle wanted to keep the babies for a few extra days to ensure a little more weight gain. Neither Sage nor Tommy wanted to leave them, but they knew it was for the best.

Tessy purposely had Tommy settle into the largest guest bedroom when they first moved in. That way there would be plenty enough room to add the two bassinets, a change table, and a comfortable chair. They soon had it arranged with everything looking cozy and restful. Sage remembered it being the same bedroom she had when she first met Tessy, who graciously invited her to stay at Ashling Manor.

Sage called her mom daily with updates. Rosemary wanted so badly to jump on a plane to meet her new granddaughters, but Rose had taken a bad fall. Nothing was broken but Rosemary felt she needed to tend to her, at least for the first week or so. Sage was very concerned about her grandmother and at the same time, disappointed her mom wasn't able to come. Rosemary promised that once she felt Rose was on the mend, she would feel comfortable enough to let Rowan and Saffron take over. She would be there as soon as she could.

For the next week, Sage and Tommy spent most of their time at the hospital. Tessy stayed vigilant for any strange energy or vibrations throughout the house. With the babies coming home soon she knew things were about to get interesting.

With Nilrem's usual flamboyant flair, he popped in often now. Both he and Tessy were on high alert. They placed a dome of protection over the bassinets but still weren't sure if that would be enough to hold off Agnes.

Tessy did a daily smudging and cleansing to ensure positive energy was prominent throughout. She kept her thoughts uplifted and pure. It really wasn't that hard considering there would soon be two precious babies in the house. That one thought alone kept her mood blissful.

Nilrem continued to drape Ashling Manor with positive orbs and energy, not to mention some Irish wit and Blessings. He wandered about the house one day with Tessy. "Maybe ye'll remember some of these, Tess." He cleared his throat and started.

"Wherever you go and whatever you do, may the luck of the Irish be there with you."

"Aye. I do remember that one." Tessy chuckled.

"Okay. How 'bout this one: As you slide down the banister of life, may the splinters never point in the wrong direction!"

Tessy laughed. "Aye, I remember my brother Keenan tellin' me that one."

"All right now, this one is for the wee poppets 'bout to arrive. May the wings of the butterfly kiss the sun. And find your shoulder to light on. To bring you luck, happiness, and riches. Today, tomorrow and beyond."

Tessy smiled. "Ah, thank ye, Nilrem. That was lovely."

With word that the twins could come home tomorrow, Nilrem decided to spend a little extra time in the babies' room.

He concentrated his energy on the bassinets and any other areas the babies would be spending most of their time. He closed his eyes, took in a deep breath and with a hand on each bassinet he literally zapped glowing auras and sparks of purple energy in and around them. The hues remained for a good while. Suddenly, he heard Sage and Tommy coming down the hall. He quickly disappeared but could do nothing about the remaining bright purple aura for a few more minutes. Before he vanished, he pointed to the doorknob to momentarily jam it. Tommy went to open the door from the other side and banged right into it. He stepped back and wriggled and jiggled the doorknob trying to get it unstuck. It took a couple of minutes before it eventually popped open with ease.

"Hmm. I'm going to have to take a look at that." He gave Sage a puzzled look.

By the time they entered the room the hues had faded.

* * *

Finally, the twins were coming home! The level of excitement throughout the house was exhilarating. Sage and Tommy literally bumped into to one another trying to finish breakfast and get out the door.

Tessy's heart was about to burst with joy. She watched as the young couple skipped down the front steps and jumped into their vehicle.

She turned to Marshall. "Oh my, just think, in a very short

while we will have those two wee darlings here, at Ashling Manor."

"Yes. It is pretty exciting, I must admit. I only hope we all still feel that way about three o'clock in the morning."

"Oh, ye stop that, now." Tessy playfully scolded, shaking her finger at him. "It will be just fine. You'll see." She tossed him a look before she turned and headed down the hall to the kitchen.

Tessy and Marshall soon had the breakfast dishes done and the kitchen clean. Marshall leaned over and kissed his wife. "Well, I guess I'll head out to the shop now. See you in a bit."

"You're what?" Tessy barked.

Marshall stepped back with surprise. "I'm sorry, is there a problem?"

"Oh sorry, love. I didn't mean to snap at ye. It's just that the kids will be home any minute with the babies and you're going to be out in the shop. Don't ye want to be here?"

Marshall huffed. "Well, darling, it's not like the babies will know. It's not like I'm never going to see them. They're living with us."

"Aye. But Sage and Tommy will know. Don't ye think they might be a bit hurt if you're not here to greet them?"

"Well, I guess. When you put it that way. Oh, all right. I'll wait then."

"Thank ye, love. I know it will make them so happy to have ye here, too."

Marshall took his paper and went into the living room while Tessy paced the front foyer. She was sure she walked a mile before she looked out the curtains and saw them pulling up the lane.

"They're here!" Tessy exclaimed, as she flung open the door.

34
Dug-up Memories

The twins settled in nicely and soon life took on a somewhat shaky but delightful schedule. Those two little darlings managed to keep four adults pretty busy. Tessy could not have felt more blessed.

Sage's mother was to arrive early next week. Rose was making great progress and Rosemary felt comfortable enough leaving her. Sage was so excited to see her but both she and Tessy were a little concerned about their unwanted guest showing up during Rosemary's visit.

It was a beautiful sunny, spring day. Sage and the babies rested comfortably. Tessy had just pulled an apple pie out of the oven and decided to escape for a while by taking a wee jaunt. She threw a warm wrap around her shoulders, slipped on her tall rubber boots, and stepped out into the spring air. Duke and Darby were immediately at her side and ready to go. They rambled off into the back grove. The path was spongy and wet but not mucky. Tessy stuck to the trail as they meandered deeper into the woods. The dogs naturally ventured off to sniff out all the glorious smells the warm weather had recently uncovered.

They had gone a fair distance when Tessy noticed Henry on the ground pecking at something. His drumming made a tinny sound. He was close to the old grain bin where Emma and Becky experienced their winter scare. Henry heard them approach and seeing the dogs, flew up and sat on the edge of the bin. Duke and Darby ran to where Henry was perched and soon there was a confrontation between the three. The dogs barked and jumped while Henry cawed and wildly flapped his wings. Tessy did her best to defuse the situation. "That's enough!" she ordered. The dogs obeyed and began to sniff around Henry's latest discovery.

Tessy pushed the dogs aside and looked on the ground. There was something glistening in the morning sun. She looked around to see if she could find a stick to dig it out. She found an odd shaped thin board and began digging, continually having to push the dogs out of the way so she could get at it. It seemed to be some type of a small cookie tin. The ground was still partly frozen. It took some effort, but she finally dug it free. She walked over to a large, felled tree and sat down. The tin was quite rusty but with a bit of force the lid popped open. Tessy leaned over to see what treasure lay buried within. The first thing she saw was a folded piece of paper. She carefully removed it and began reading aloud, "Time Capsule 1968. Lilian Scott and Maggie Blewett."

"Blessed be!" Tessy exhaled. She dug deeper into the tin and pulled out sweet treasures that a child would cherish. Wrapped in a lacy hankie was a small kewpie-doll with a feather in her hair. The kind you'd win at the fair. There were six marbles, all Cat's Eyes. A couple of painted rocks, a seashell, and a handful of dried up rose petals. The last two items were bubble gum comics. Tessy smiled.

She carefully placed the items back in the tin and secured the lid, then sat for a minute. She wondered where those lovely children, with such fun and adventure in their hearts, could be now? Then it hit her. The Scott family lived at Ashling Manor before Tessy had even moved to Ladyslipper.

"And, hmm," she said aloud to Henry and the dogs. "Maggie Blewett. Blewett. I should know that name." Tessy's eyes flew wide open. "Oh, my stars! Henry, Duke, Darby! Maggie Blewett is Margaret Chamberlain." The animals stared at her with a blank expression. "Can ye imagine Mrs. Chamberlain as a happy child?"

What she did know is that she should return the tin to Mrs. Chamberlain, as she had no idea where the Scott's lived now.

Tessy rushed back to the house, changed into some shoes, and grabbed the car keys. She wasn't sure how Mrs. Chamberlain would greet her, but she had to go and go now.

It was a short drive and once she arrived at the house she pulled into the driveway and shut off the engine. She took in a long, deep breath before she got out of the car. She marched up the front walk with the tin in hand and tapped on the door. It took a few minutes before Mrs. Chamberlain opened it. She glared at Tessy.

"What are you doing here?" she snipped.

"Good day, Margaret. I believe I have something here you might be interested in." Tessy glanced down at the tin, then raised it slightly.

Mrs. Chamberlain looked at it with furrowed brows. "What

is it?" She studied it for a moment. The second she recognized it she turned pale.

"Margaret! Are ye all right?" Tessy took Mrs. Chamberlain by the hand. "Come, sit out on the step a minute."

Uncharacteristically, Mrs. Chamberlain did as she was told. She stepped out and sat down on the top step. She held out her hand for the tin. Tessy handed it to her.

"Where did you get this?" Mrs. Chamberlain softly asked. Tessy had never heard such tenderness in her voice before.

"I discovered it on my walk this morning." Tessy watched Mrs. Chamberlain's face. "It was buried near an old grain bin in my back grove."

"Yes, I remember." Mrs. Chamberlain smiled, then went quiet. She pried the tin open and peered in. Her smile widened.

Tessy wasn't sure if she should stay or whether she should leave Mrs. Chamberlain to her memories in private. Before she could make a firm decision, Mrs. Chamberlain started to talk.

"Lilian was my best friend way back then."

Tessy could see she had drifted into childhood memories.

"I'm sure you find it hard to believe that I actually had a best friend, but I did and we were inseparable," she continued.

Tessy remained quiet and let her go on.

"I probably know the inside of your house as well as you. Lilian and her older sister had the large bedroom overlooking the backyard. On rainy days, we would play house for hours up in the attic. But mostly we played in that back grove. There wasn't so much underbrush back then and the trees weren't so tall, but it was heaven to us."

Margaret looked inside the tin and began to pull out the childhood memories. She laughed. A tender laugh that Tessy had never heard before. She unwrapped the Kewpie-doll and stroked her thumb over it.

"We won this at the fair. We each got one, but her dog ate mine. Lilian felt bad and gave me hers. She was like that. So kind and generous. I thought it only right that it go into our time capsule." She spotted the marbles and laughed again. "These were our lucky Cat's Eyes. When we played marbles with the other kids, we won with these same six every time." She dumped the remaining contents into her lap, then scooped up the dried rose petals and instinctively raised them to her face while drawing in a breath. "Mmm, these were freshly picked that day. No smell left, now." She looked down. "These were our pet rocks. Can't remember their names." She looked off in the distance and chuckled.

She looked down again and picked up the shell. "Lilian brought this back for me when she and her family went to the ocean for holidays one summer." Finally, Margaret unfolded the bubble gum comics and read them. She smiled. "The day we buried this tin we had previously gone down to Mrs. Butterworth's candy store. She gave us each a Bubblicious before we left. All the way home we tried to see who could blow the biggest bubble. Lilian loved Bubblicious. She said if pink had a flavour that's what it would be." Margaret laughed.

Tessy was intrigued by Margaret's precise recollection of each and every item. "What precious memories," Tessy whispered, feeling compelled to pat Margaret's hand.

Mrs. Chamberlain looked up at Tessy with tears in her eyes. She continued on with her story. "We buried the tin in late spring, right before Lilian got really sick. She'd had a bad winter with colds and infections. We all thought that once the nice weather came, she would get better and stronger. She didn't. They took her to the doctor and that's when they told me she had leukemia. I had no idea what that word meant at the time. What it did end up meaning to me was the last of the happiest days of my life.

"Lilian believed in God, in faeries and unicorns, and things like your magick. She stayed happy and lovely and never gave up on those forces. Yet, not one of them helped her. Not one bit! I watched my best friend wither and die."

She slammed the tin down on the step. The Mrs. Chamberlain Tessy had grown accustomed to, resurfaced.

"I never allowed myself to ever get that attached to anyone again," she continued. Then to Tessy's surprise, her expression softened again. "I'm sorry. Thank you for bringing me the tin. I'm not sure why I told you all this. Just forget about it." She picked up the tin and stood to go back in the house.

"Margaret, please. Wait. Thank you for sharing those lovely memories with me. I'm truly honoured. And please know, that God never once gave up on Lilian. Some souls just aren't meant to spend much time on Earth but what time they do have they give with their whole heart. That is what Lilian gave you. That's the magick."

Mrs. Chamberlain looked at Tessy, lowered her head, then silently turned and went in her house, closing the door behind her.

Tessy got up and returned to her car. All the way home she processed the illuminating encounter she'd just experienced. After all these years, Tessy finally had a deeper understanding of where Margaret's anger and intolerance came from. Her childhood best friend had sadly been taken and she had no control over it. She felt betrayed by God and the magick Lilian held inside her. Margaret never healed from the traumatic experience and that's what left her so bitter and tainted.

Tessy secretly hoped these shared tender moments with Margaret might, somehow, be a new beginning for the two of them. She was, however, not going to hold her breath.

35
The Evil that Lurks Within

Tessy was deep in thought after her visit with Mrs. Chamberlain as she pulled into the lane of Ashling Manor. When she reached the garage, she saw Henry on the roof creating quite a commotion. She heard his cawing before she even got out of the car. She stepped out and stood below him.

"Henry, dear! What in the devil is the matter?"

He flew over, landed on the back porch, and continued to make a fuss.

Tessy stepped into the porch. Duke and Darby greeted her with their hackles up. They turned facing towards the inside door and growled. Tessy immediately felt the dark presence and a strong stench hovering in the air. She locked the dogs in the porch and flew up to Sage's room. She flung open the door and there was Agnes standing over Willow's bassinet. Sage was still sleeping. Tessy intuitively thrust out her hand towards Agnes and watched her crash against the wall. Tessy was as shocked as Agnes.

Agnes's screech and the heavy thud woke Sage with a start. The babies also woke and started to cry. Sage's first instinct was to rush to her children. Agnes slowly picked herself up and moved closer into the room. She growled and hissed towards the Mother and Crone.

"Sage, I need ye to stand directly across from me. Right there." Tessy pointed to a spot on the far side of the room. "Are you wearing the amulet?"

"Yes. But I don't know what I'm doing," she cried.

"Sage, you are going to put into practise what ye have learned to protect your children. All the things we've been preparing ye for." Tessy calmly answered while she continued to hold Agnes at bay with her stare and an outstretched arm. "Now, hold the amulet up towards Agnes."

Sage's courage was empowered with the energy of a thousand gifted Celtic ancestors. It burst into her soul, guiding and assisting her to take down this evil demon. "You're right! Let's do this!" Sage confidently grinned, as she held up the inherited treasure toward Agnes.

Tessy then called out, "Nilrem. T'would be a good time for ye to pop in, dear. But, please, let's keep the theatrics down to maybe just one snap, crackle or pop."

With one mighty burst of purple, Nilrem appeared.

"Thank you, Nilrem. Now, if you could please take your spot, as discussed."

Nilrem carefully moved in behind Agnes. They now held her captive in a triangle, a vortex of sorts. Tessy raised her hand. As she air traced the outline of the triangle with her finger, a thick pouring of salt appeared to complete the invisible wall of protection. When she finished, a quick flick of her hand produced lit candles at intervals throughout.

With hearing all the commotion, Marshall and Tommy

raced upstairs and into the room. They stopped dead at the sight before them. The temperature in the room had dropped so dramatically it caused them both to shudder. Tessy did not break her stance from holding Agnes and without turning she instructed Marshall.

"I would like ye and Tommy to take the babies. Take them outside or take them for a drive but, please, take them straight away. Then, wait to hear from me."

Tommy started to object. "Sage, what the hell is going on? Who is this? I'm not leaving you."

"Tommy," Sage pleaded. "I need you to do as Tessy asks. Please. I'll explain everything later."

Tessy continued, "Tommy, are ye still wearing that chain with the ring?"

"Yes," he answered.

"Good. Do not take it off. Take the wee ones and go. Please!"

Marshall pulled Tommy aside. "I think we need to get the babies out of here, right now. I'll fill you in on as much as I know. Come on." Marshall and Tommy did as they were instructed and left the room with the little girls in hand.

Agnes became more and more agitated. She made hideous sounds as she tried to move throughout the vortex. Her aura seeped and dripped dark greys and putrid greens all around her.

As Tessy predicted, there was no need to summon any destructive forces. The demons Agnes housed within her own mind appeared and were more than terrifying enough. They oozed out of her like deep, infected wounds. Agnes, unable to escape her own horrors, dodged and swatted at the images entangling around her body.

Now, was the time for Tessy to call in the angels, guides and all others to assist in helping Agnes cross over to the Otherside.

She spoke aloud and with great respect. "We call upon and welcome Archangel Michael in our time of need. Please use your mighty sword to cut away any unhealthy attachments, evil cords or ties still binding and holding back Agnes Haggerty. Shower her with your brilliant healing and help her move into the light.

"We call upon and welcome Archangel Azrael in our time of need. We ask that you help Agnes Haggerty to confront her pain so she may cope and thrive. We also ask, as your primary role, to assist and guide Agnes in peacefully crossing over into the light.

"We call upon and welcome all others wishing to be here today in helping Agnes Haggerty move into the light and peacefully cross over."

Moments later the room was filled with a warmth and blinding, brilliant light. The feeling of peace and love in the room invaded every inch of space. Agnes cried out and threw her arm up over her eyes. The light faded a little, still bright, but no longer blinding. Tessy, Sage, and Nilrem held their positions and watched in reverence.

Agnes slowly moved her arm away from her face. Michael, who stood tall and handsome, smiled at her with such warmth that Agnes was paralyzed. In silence, he took his sword and cut away all the poison and evil that surrounded her. It dropped and melted into the light of pure love.

Azrael stepped close to Agnes and held her head in his hands to remove her remaining turmoil and pain. A tunnel of white light stretched across the back of the vortex. There were two little girls standing at the far end beckoning Agnes to come. Agnes looked deep down into the tunnel. Tears rolled down her cheeks and she bitterly cried out to them over and over again, "I'm sorry. I'm so sorry."

Tessy realized the two little girls were Agnes's twin sisters who had died in the fire. All of a sudden it became clear. She called out to Agnes. "Agnes, those are the Haggerty twins that have been lovingly haunting ye all these years. Ye were never meant to be with Keenan and I, nor with our wee Willow and Poppy. 'Twas your very own Haggerty twin sisters that have been calling ye home. Go. Go to them, now."

Agnes looked straight at Tessy. Another little girl appeared and stood beside Agnes. She emerged wrapped in pure radiance. She smiled up at Agnes and took her hand. They started walking toward the tunnel.

Azrael took Agnes's other arm and guided her along. They stopped at the tunnel entrance. Agnes needed to be the one to take that first step in. It had to be of her own free will.

The world stood still. It seemed like forever. Agnes saw her little sisters lovingly outstretch their arms to her. She took the step.

Tessy, Sage, and Nilrem all sighed in relief. They watched Agnes, the little girl and Azrael walk down the tunnel into the light. When Agnes hugged her sisters, she looked back to Tessy.

Her face, at long last, was filled with peace instead of torment and scars. Tessy thanked all those who had appeared and assisted. The tunnel faded, the light disappeared, and the guestroom went back to its normal state, as if nothing had ever happened.

The three of them collapsed onto the bed physically exhausted, yet emotionally exhilarated.

"Wow! What the hell was that!" Sage exploded.

"That, my dear, was a combination of magick and a miracle." Tessy laughed.

Nilrem chuckled. "All in a day's work for a magician, my dear. Feels grand to dust off the old wand and get back down to business. See, I told ye, Tessy, I knew we could stop her in her tracks."

"Well, we wouldn't have been able to do it without a lot of help from Sage and those blessed angels," Tessy added. "I wonder who the other little girl was?" There was a moment of silence before Tessy's eyes flew open.

"What?" Sage asked.

"I know exactly who that was." Tessy smiled. "That was sweet wee Lilian. This used to be her bedroom."

"What?" Sage repeated. "This house is haunted? Who's Lilian?"

Tessy laughed. "I wouldn't call it haunted. Lilian's family used to live here, then she died. They moved away but Lilian must have decided to stay. I've often thought I felt another presence other than Dermot. How wonderful!"

Sage gaped at Tessy. "Seriously?"

Tessy laughed again. "I wouldn't bother mentioning Lilian to Tommy or Marshall. I'm thinking that should remain our little secret."

36
A Scolding and New Beginnings

Tessy sent Marshall a text to let him know all was clear and it was safe to return. She and Sage sat at the kitchen table savouring a congratulatory cup of tea. Nilrem had since popped off but assured, "I'll not be far," before he left.

"Well, my dear, I would say ye have passed your Wise Woman initiation with flying colours." Tessy proudly complimented Sage as she raised her teacup high in the air.

Sage laughed. "That was some initiation! Sure hope I won't ever have to do that again."

"Aye. I agree with ye, there, love."

Marshall and Tommy soon returned home, each carrying a wee girl. The twins were sound asleep all snug and safe in their car seats. Sage jumped up to check on her sweet babies. Tommy did not look happy.

"You two have some explaining to do." He frowned at his wife then glanced over to Tessy.

Sage touched his arm. "Honey, I'm sorry. How could I tell you? You never would have believed it. Hell, I had a hard time believing it."

Tessy stood and pulled out a chair. "Tommy, dear. Please, come sit."

Tommy complied and walked over to the table and sat down.

"Marshall told me what he knew but I couldn't fathom what he was saying."

"See!" Sage said. "I knew you'd have a hard time understanding."

"Really? Do you think an, I told you so, is helping right at this moment?" Tommy glared. "Our daughters were in danger!"

"I'm sorry. I didn't mean it like that. You're right."

Tessy decided to intervene. "Tommy, I agree, there was a risk to the babies. However, there had been plenty of warning ahead of time and I, and then we," she pointed at Sage, "took every precaution to ensure the safety of our wee Willow and Poppy. We also had help from another realm and beyond."

"That's the other thing," spat Tommy. "Who the hell was that, that, that, whatever he was? Not to mention the monster that stood in the centre of you guys."

"I'll do my best to tell ye from the very beginnin', dear." Tessy sat close and cited her tale. "It all started forty years ago, back in Ireland, when Keenan and I lost our parents."

Tessy carried on and told the whole tragic story from beginning to end. She hoped, somehow, Tommy would have a better understanding of why and what led up to the disturbing event he had witnessed. When she finished, Tommy sat quiet.

It took a few minutes, but Tommy lifted his head towards Tessy. "I'm sorry you have lived through so much pain for so long. I still have no idea what went on here today but at least, I now know why. I always knew there was something really special about you Tessy. Yes, even magickal." He chuckled. "And, Sage,

I know you have the same Haggerty gift. I guess I'm just going to have to learn to live with this magick and all the other weird stuff that goes along with it."

Sage got up from her chair and wrapped her arms around Tommy's neck and kissed him. "Thank you, sweetheart. I promise I will never keep anything from you again." With that statement, she immediately wondered what to do about Lilian. Then she concluded that in all actuality, as far as she knew, Lilian was no longer physically in the house. There, all better.

"Okay. You'd better not. I'm sorry I got so mad." They kissed again.

Tessy smiled at the loving couple, and then quipped, "Well, by all accounts, ye and Marshall were the ones to actually remove the babies from harm's way. So ye two are the real heroes."

"Yah, yah. Okay, you don't need to butter us up. We forgive you two magickal warriors." Marshall laughed. "However, I think after all this I need something a little stronger than a tea. How 'bout a beer, Tommy? I know I could use one."

"Boy, I'm with ya. That sounds good."

Sage smiled and shook her head at her husband. "Okay, but before you open your beer could you please help me change the girls and get them ready for a feeding?"

Tessy waved her hand in the air. "Ye boys go on ahead. I'll help Sage with the wee ones."

* * *

While all was forgiven between the adults, the two wee

Haggerty twins lay snug and warm with full tummies, sound asleep in their bassinets. Sage tip-toed out of their room and gently closed the door behind her.

She found Tessy in the kitchen preparing a lovely salmon loaf for supper. The guys were in the living room watching the hockey game. On the way by, Sage poked her head in to see who was winning before she carried on into the kitchen to help Tessy with supper.

Tessy was quiet, deep in thought, when Sage walked in. Sage looked at her and went over and put an arm around her. "Are you okay?" she asked.

"Aye, love, I am. I truly am, now. I'm so relieved to have all that nasty business over with. Knowing I don't have to fret and worry over keeping those sweet, wee poppets safe."

"Yah. It's almost like a bad dream now. I guess that's kinda what it was." Sage concluded, as she pulled plates out of the cupboard.

"Aye. Thankfully, we can both put those bad dreams behind us. Blessed be!"

"Yes." Sage heartedly agreed, as she placed the cutlery on the table. She stood quiet for a moment, then looked over at Tessy. "Thank you so much for being who you are, Tessy. I don't even want to imagine what could have happened if you weren't as gifted and powerful as you are." Sage shuddered.

"Ahh, love. It took our combined gifts to help Agnes take that journey. Ye are just as gifted and have as much power inside ye, maybe even more. Ye just have to practice and stay confident in your abilities. That goes for everything in your life."

Sage gave Tessy a hug and continued to set the table. Moments later, the guys appeared at the door ready to eat.

While everyone sat, laughing and talking around the supper table, Willow and Poppy lay dreaming while breathing out sweet, contented whimpers. Not one adult gave a thought to the special gifts these wee ones might possess. They were of Haggerty blood, being raised by a gifted Mother and living in the house of a gifted Crone. The possibilities were endless.

The baby's room quietly filled with a soft hue of purple as Nilrem appeared. He stood between the bassinets and smiled into one, then the other. He reached into baby Willow's bassinet and lightly brushed his hand over her soft brow. "May Irish blessings and good health be upon ye all of yer days." Then he repeated the same blessing to Poppy. "May Irish Blessings and good health be upon ye all of yer days."

Nilrem stayed for a while cooing over them and humming an Irish lullaby. When it was time for him to leave, he blew them each a kiss and sprinkled some purple hue over them. And with that, he was gone.

Back at the dinner table, Tessy smiled. She felt his energy leave and noticed purple sparkles dancing about everyone seated before her. Nilrem had returned to his realm, but she knew he would never be far off.

While the babies slept, Tessy and Marshall cleared the table. Then Tessy brought out a warm apple pie. Marshall had barely taken a bite when they heard a soft tapping at the front door.

Tessy looked at everyone, raised her eyebrows, then headed to the foyer. She peeked out the curtains to see Mrs. Chamberlain on her doorstep. She opened the door.

"Well, good evenin' Margaret," Tessy said. "Please come in."

"Good evening. No, thanks, I really can't stay. I just wanted to drop off a couple of gifts for the babies."

"How lovely. Thank ye. Just one minute and I'll get Sage and Tommy."

"No, really, that's not necessary." Mrs. Chamberlain stated, but it was too late. Tessy had already called out to the kids.

A slightly uncomfortable Mrs. Chamberlain waited at the door and watched Sage and Tommy hurry down the hall. Marshall wasn't far behind.

As soon as Sage saw who it was, she slowed her pace. "Oh hello, Mrs. Chamberlain."

"Hello, Sage. Tommy." Their guest nodded. "I didn't mean to bother you. I just wanted to drop off these little gifts for the babies." She handed them to Sage.

"Well, thank you so much. How thoughtful of you." Sage looked up at Tommy and smiled.

"Yes, thank you," Tommy added.

"You're welcome. Well, I'll let you get back to whatever you were doing. Congratulations to you both." And with that, she turned and left.

As they all made their way back into the kitchen, Marshall piped, "What the heck was that all about. She certainly has taken a turn for the better."

Tessy didn't feel right betraying Margaret's trust with sharing her intimate memories. She replied, "Well, I don't want say too much but she and I had a wee visit today. And, I'm thinkin' we just may have had a slight breakthrough in our relationship. I'm hoping so, anyway."

"Well, whatever. It was very nice of her to bring the babies a gift." Sage beamed.

Tessy put her arm around Sage. "Aye, it certainly was. Now, who's ready for more dessert and tea?"

It had been a big day. Tessy glanced around the table at the people she loved. Her heart overflowed with joy and gratitude.

Tessy lay in bed later that night, thankful for how everything turned out. She was grateful for the wisdom and magickal gifts she'd been blessed with. How her mother, and all Mothers and Crones before her, had guarded and passed down the Craft for future generations to treasure.

Knowing she, too, had recently passed on such wisdom did her heart good. She knew it would continue to be well-guarded and practiced with love and respect. Sage would see to that.

* * *

With all forgiven, things went back to the wonderful life of baby coos and cuddles. Sage's mom was arriving in a few hours and Sage was ecstatic. She couldn't wait to show off her darling daughters. Tommy had to go to work, but Sage promised to take plenty of pictures to record the momentous reunion for him.

The babies were fed, bathed, and put down for an early nap so they would be fresh and in fine form to meet Grandma for the first time.

By the time Rosemary arrived Tessy was just as excited and anxious as Sage. When she saw the rented vehicle pull up the lane, she flung open the front door and flew out onto the step to greet her. Sage was not far behind.

"Welcome! Welcome!" Tessy hailed as Rosemary opened the car door and stepped out.

"Mom!" Sage cried and ran past Tessy to hug her mother.

The two hugged and rocked longer than a minute before they separated to have a good look at one another. Rosemary touched Sage's face gently with the palm of her hand before kissing her on the cheek.

"Oh darling. You look wonderful. Motherhood agrees with you."

"Thanks, Mom. You look great, too."

Tessy joined the two and she and Rosemary hugged.

"How was your trip, dear?" Tessy asked.

"Uneventful. So good." Rosemary laughed.

"Grand. Now, leave your bags. Marshall said he'd come out and fetch them for ye. Come. I'm sure ye could use a cup of tea."

"What I'm really anxious for is to see my grandchildren!"

Sage laughed. "They're still sleeping but they should be up and going any minute now."

"Oooh, I hope so." Rosemary frowned.

"Well, how 'bout I take you up to their room and you can at

least have a peek," Sage offered.

"Yes! Please."

Rosemary stood over one bassinet and then the other with tears in her eyes. She put her hand over her heart, shook her head, then looked at Sage with true love and pride.

On their way to the kitchen Rosemary commented she couldn't wait much longer to hold her granddaughters. She soon got her wish. They had barely sat down to tea when they heard little gurgles and grumbles coming from the baby monitor that sat on the kitchen counter. All three ladies leapt off their chairs and headed for the stairway. Sage was in the lead when they reached the bedroom: but not by much.

Sage picked up Willow and handed her to Rosemary. "Mom, I'd like you to meet Willow Rose. Willow, darling, this is your grandma."

"Well, hello, sweet Willow. Grandma is so excited to finally meet you." Rosemary gazed down at the little face as it stared back with bewilderment. "Oh my gosh! She is so alert!" Rosemary exclaimed.

"Yes. They both are but Willow, even at three weeks, doesn't seem to miss a thing," Sage boasted.

As Sage lifted Poppy, Rosemary kissed Willow on the head and handed her to Tessy.

"And this little rascal is Poppy June. Poppy, meet your grandma."

The second Rosemary took her, she tooted in her pants, smiled, and wrinkled up her tiny nose. Everyone laughed.

"Yep. That's our Poppy." Sage shook her head and reached towards her mother so she could take her back and change her.

Tessy stood quietly and relished in these special moments that had taken place. Whether she realized it or not, Rosemary had just taken on the blessed role of Crone. This was a life of new beginnings for them all.

By the end of two joyful weeks, Rosemary was able to easily distinguish between the girls with no problem. Willow had Sage's alabaster skin colour with red hair while Poppy was a bit smaller and more like Tommy. Her olive skin, darker hair and personality set her apart. Dozens of pictures were taken, numerous matching outfits were bought, and millions of baby kisses were given. Before they knew it, Rosemary stood in the driveway saying her tearful goodbyes. She felt tearing herself away from her precious granddaughters was the toughest ordeal she had ever encountered.

"Now, promise you'll Skype me at least once a week so I can see how much they are growing."

"Yes, of course, Mom." Sage was holding Poppy, crying, and having just as hard a time saying goodbye.

Tessy had already said her goodbyes. She stood close by holding Willow and shed a few tears of her own. She felt heartbroken for them both.

Rosemary rushed over and kissed each baby one more time before hugging Sage and climbing into the car. She wiped her tears and drove off.

Sage walked over to Tessy and had one more good cry before

they turned and went into Ashling Manor. Tears dried and life carried on.

Days turned into weeks. Tessy was glad the nightmares were over, the danger had passed, and life had a beautiful, natural way about it again. She had convinced the kids to stay on for a while longer. She secretly hoped forever.

One night, Tessy lay awake, pondering the events of the last month. In the quiet and darkness of her bedroom she revelled in knowing that two sweet, twin poppets lay cozy just down the hall. They were safe and loved, each unique with their own dash and hue of magick. This gave her great peace of mind. She felt her life was complete and this was her time for new beginnings.

37
Five Years Later

Spring's brilliant sun gaily beamed onto Tessy and Marshall's cheery cottage porch. Their elderly dog, Duke, lay stretched against the railing, soaking up the afternoon's warmth. Tessy and Sage enjoyed afternoon tea while watching the twins play hide and seek in the yard.

"My, it's hard to believe Willow and Poppy have turned five already. Where did the time go? Seems like only yesterday ye brought those wee poppets home from the hospital." Tessy wondered aloud.

"I know. Tommy and I ask ourselves that all the time. I'm not sure how we would have managed if you hadn't insisted we continue to stay on at Ashling Manor. I still don't think it was necessary for you and Marshall to build this cottage. There was plenty of room for us all. I've always felt like we kicked you out of your own home."

"Nonsense dear. Ye did nothing of the kind. Ashling Manor was becoming too much for Marshall and me. And, besides, it needed to be filled with family. It was our idea to build this sweet wee cottage back here near the trees. It's just perfect for us. We're right here to help out in any way we can but we still each have our privacy. It works out just grand."

"Well, you know Ashling Manor will always be your home

and you can come and go as you please."

"Aye dear, thank ye. I know."

Poppy ran up and plunked herself down on the top step. She gently stroked Duke's head. "Auntie Tess?"

"Aye, love."

"Why won't Duke play with us anymore?"

"Well dear, Duke is pretty old and tired. He's done a lot of running and playing in his long life."

"Is he going to die like Darby did?"

"Aye. He will someday. And, probably not too long from now."

"That makes me sad. I'm going to miss him."

"Aye, me too, Poppy, dear, me too." Tessy looked down at what has been her constant companion for over ten years. Her eyes welled at the thought of having to say goodbye one day soon.

Sage broke the tender moment. "Poppy, where's Willow?"

"Still hiding, I guess."

"Poppy!" Her mother scolded, shaking her head. "You go find her."

"Well, she'll come out 'ventually." Poppy shrugged.

"Young lady. Now, please."

"Oh, all right," Poppy grumbled as she slowly got up, gave Duke one more pet and meandered off.

"Thank you," her mother called after her.

Neither Sage nor Tessy could hide their amusement.

"That Poppy is such a character." Tessy laughed. "Like a fart in the wind."

Sage joined in on Tessy's laughter. "Boy, you can say that again."

"And wee Willow, such a serious, contemplating child. And my, what a little mother she's become." Tessy beamed.

"Oh yes, they are as different as night and day! Willow certainly does like to boss around, what she calls, her little sister."

"Oh, but she would protect Poppy to the ends of the earth and back."

"Yes, she would. They are both very protective of one another. I couldn't be more pleased."

"Or more blessed." Tessy cooed.

"Yes, I agree. Tommy and I have been blessed."

The phone rang and they looked at one another.

"Do you need to get that?" Sage asked.

"No. Marshall is in the house. He'll get it."

Tessy could hear Marshall's part of the conversation through the screen door. "It sounds like it's Dotty and Bert," she mused out loud.

"How do they like having total control over the B&B now that they have purchased it from you and Marshall."

"They seem to be loving it more and more every time we talk. Marshall and I haven't been to visit in some time, but we are planning a trip to Winnipeg within the next month or so."

"Are they staying busy with it?"

"Aye. I think they were booked solid this past Christmas then, again, in February during the Festival du Voyageur."

"That's wonderful. Marshall's not missing it too much?"

"Not one bit! Between ye and I, I believe he is so relieved not to have to deal with it anymore. He hasn't whispered a word about it since the takeover. And he's so much happier, lately."

"Well, that's good. He's supposed to be retired." Sage laughed. "Are Dotty and Bert planning on keeping the name, The Doctor's Inn?"

"Aye. They are. To them it will always be Dr. Tayse's residence, and they would keep the name to honour him."

"Ahh, that's so sweet."

"Aye. I agree, 'tis."

Marshall came out onto the porch with that charming, boyish grin Tessy had never been able to resist.

"Well now, don't ye look like the cat that caught the canary." Tessy giggled.

"Well, I just got confirmation on a little surprise I have been planning." Marshall boasted, chest out and head high.

Before he could continue, a squabble between Willow and Poppy broke out.

"Oh dear. I think they may need a time-out. Excuse me." Sage quickly rose and ran out to referee.

Tessy and Marshall stood and watched Sage calm and herd the girls towards the manor. She turned before they went into the house and waved goodbye to them. They chuckled and waved back.

"Oh, those wee rascals. They do keep their mam busy." Tessy smiled.

"They certainly do," Marshall agreed.

"Now, what was it ye were wantin' to say, love?"

"Oh, right. Well, my darling. I have booked us into The Doctor's Inn for a week. And all five of my kids and their spouses are booked in for that week, too!"

"Oh, my stars! How wonderful. How did ye accomplish that?"

"Well, I've been working on it for a while now. We finally found a few days that coincided, and it just happened."

They chatted on about the mini holiday for a time. Marshall was understandably excited and Tessy was so happy to hear him prattle on. The last time they had all been together was at Tessy and Marshall's wedding over seven years ago. Marshall had every right to be excited.

About an hour later, Tessy heard a tap at the cottage door. She looked out the screen to see two little faces smiling up at her.

"Well, hello, my wee darlings. Come in. Come in. Are ye feeling a mite better now?"

"Yes," they chimed. They pulled open the screen door and let it slam shut as they rushed in.

"Grand."

"Mommy made us have some quiet time and then we had to apologize to one another," Willow reported.

"Well, that was nice. Don't ye find getting along makes life easier?"

"I guess." Poppy shrugged.

Willow gave her sister a motherly glare. "Yes, it does, Poppy. Right?"

"Okay. Yes, it does." Poppy teasingly glared back at her.

"Auntie Tess?" asked Willow.

"Aye, love."

"Are you making any lotions or potions today?"

Tessy chuckled. "Well, I suppose I could. Is there something special you'd like to make?"

"Not really, we just wanna help you."

"All right, my dears. How 'bout we make a lotion for cuts and scrapes and bumps and bruises?"

"Yeah." The little girls jumped up and down.

"Well then, let's go to the little back kitchen at Ashling Manor and see what we can find to mix up." Tessy picked up a basket for the ingredients and hand in hand the three marched across the lawn and into Ashling Manor.

They spent the afternoon at the cottage measuring, mixing, sniffing oils and herbs while they chatted about faeries and unicorns.

Tessy could not have felt more blessed. The Crone innocently shared the Craft with two wee maidens. They were learning their inherited Gift through play, and play was all they realized for now.

The two wee girls went home for supper, each proudly carrying their very own jar of scratch and scrape lotion. Tessy stood at the screen door and watched them until they disappeared into Ashling Manor.

Marshall nestled up behind her and hugged her waist.

"How 'bout we take Brigid for a spin and I'll treat you to dinner out at our favourite restaurant?"

"Oh my. Do ye mean the restaurant where we had our first date? The Inner Peace Bistro?"

"The very same."

"Sounds wonderful. What did I do to deserve such a man?" Tessy turned and hugged her husband's neck.

"Just lucky, I guess." Marshall winked and kissed his wife.

As they slowly drove out of town and towards Ladyslipper Lake, Tessy knew she was way more than lucky. *Truly blessed,* were the thoughts of the Wise Woman: *truly blessed.*

Blessed be.

Acknowledgements

A huge thank you to the following people:

I would like to reiterate some of my past words of gratitude to my wonderful editor/publisher, Darcy Nybo, of Always Write / Artistic Warrior Publishing. Your tireless energy, natural talent, knowledge, encouragement and humour are a well that never runs dry. You tell me how good I am getting at this writing stuff, well, I feel a big part of that is because of the classes I have taken from you through Always Write. You are my teacher/mentor, turned friend, and I truly appreciate all that you have taught me. You are a treasure. Darcy also authored two books of short stories and several children's books.

Great appreciation goes to Judah Tyreman. He suggested his talented father, Chris Tyreman, design this magickal book cover for me. I wanted something to reflect Tessy's best-loved time of year, autumn. And, wow, what a perfect image he created. I couldn't have imagined anything better.

Thank you to all my beta readers. Where would I be without you? The first person to always read my manuscripts is my sister, Diane. She also takes on the role of my confidant, sounding board, shoulder to cry on and my best friend. It's a pretty tall order but she handles it well.

Next to read my book, was my dear friend, Deb Runnalls. She is so encouraging, kind and always fills my heart with joy.

Then Darlene Stevenson, wow, where do I begin? Darlene is

so thorough, talented and asks a thousand needed questions. I think she missed her calling as an excellent editor! She first read it in its rough form and then again in its polished edition; such a trooper.

And last to read it, but by no means least, Audrey Magnusson. Audrey is a fan and has read all my other books, so I really appreciate her input. It's always a delight to hear what a reader has to say. This is the second time both Darlene and Audrey have beta read for me.

A special thank you goes to Jonas Saul for the final proofread of my book. Jonas is the bestselling author of the Sarah Roberts Series and has written and published around forty thriller novels so far. I am truly honoured and appreciate your tips, suggestions and kind words. They will follow me throughout my writing career.

To my son, Rob, for your encouragement and assistance with, every author's nightmare: marketing. Your patience during the countless hours of trying to teach me how not to be technically challenged has been an uphill battle. And, we're not there yet. It's a good thing you love me.

To my brother Craig and his wife, Karen, my beautiful, blended family, many dear friends and kindred spirits thank you for your continuous encouragement, support and loving energy. The constant interest and enquiries from the faithful readers of Tessy McGuigan is overwhelming and none of this would happen without you. You are all a huge part of this magickal journey that keeps Tessy alive. Thank you.

About the Author

Elaine Gugin Maddex is a wife, mother, grandmother, and author. She was born and raised in the charming town of Minnedosa, Manitoba.

As a small child she would follow her grandmother and help out in her massive gardens. (It was more than likely that she just got under foot.) This experience left a huge imprint on her life and the country girl remained.

She is a kitchen herbalist who loves concocting herbal remedies. In her spare time you can find her enjoying special moments with family, pets and friends, and on the road, promoting her books and doing readings.

To book Elaine for an author reading, please email her at: guginmaddex@gmail.com

These books, by Elaine Gugin Maddex, are all available on Amazon.

More Than a Wise Woman

Wise Woman's Manor

Wise Woman's Homage